There is no shadow withou[t]
— H[...]

SYSTEMA PARADOXA

ACCOUNTS OF CRYPTOZOOLOGICAL IMPORT

VOLUME 12
THE PLAY OF LIGHT
A TALE OF THE SHADOW PEOPLE

AS ACCOUNTED BY DANIELLE ACKLEY-MCPHAIL

NEOPARADOXA
Pennsville, NJ
2022

PUBLISHED BY
NeoParadoxa
A division of eSpec Books
PO Box 242
Pennsville, NJ 08070
www.especbooks.com

Copyright © 2022 Danielle Ackley-McPhail

ISBN: 978-1-949691-57-3
ISBN (ebook): 978-1-949691-56-6

All rights reserved. No part of the contents of this book may be reproduced or transmitted in any form or by any means without the written permission of the publisher.

All persons, places, and events in this book are fictitious and any resemblance to actual persons, places, or events is purely coincidental.

Interior Design: Danielle McPhail
www.sidhenadaire.com

Cover Art: Jason Whitley
Cover Design: Mike and Danielle McPhail, McP Digital Graphics
Interior Illustration: Jason Whitley

Copyediting: Greg Schauer, John L. French, and Dale Russell

Dedication

To Moe Oresin and Matt Gorton, for setting us on this journey

Chapter One

Just before seven a.m., Sheridan Cascaden stood on the curb staring at the blue ranch-style farmhouse she had grown up in. The structure seemed more worn and faded but otherwise unchanged. Not for the first time, she wondered why she hadn't opted to stay at the local B&B. Five years had passed since she'd been home, her visit transitioning from "long overdue" to "possibly too late" in the dark hours of the morning two days ago when her cell phone rang, waking her. Ribbons of guilt and unease coiled over and around one another in her belly.

Enough nonsense. You're getting worked up over nothing, she thought, going for stern, but lacking conviction even to herself. Memories kept edging closer, pushing at the barriers she held tight against them. Memories of a time all too similar to now.

As if reacting to her inner conflict, the shadow-dappled front walk seemed to mimic movement where there should be none. Her common sense recognized that the breeze swayed the trees standing sentinel in the yard, but part of her denied that logic, searching for living forms among the leaf shadow. She jerked her gaze away from the shifting patterns and settled it on the front door. Drawing a bracing breath, she lifted the latch on the chain-link gate and pushed it open. Her shoulders tensed at the shrill squeak, but she did not move up the walk.

She meant to.
She needed to.
…She couldn't.
The heart had gone out of her childhood home.

At her back, the taxi driver pointedly cleared his throat. Sheridan jumped, her deep crimson locks twirling about her shoulders as she looked behind her with a faint frown. He stood there holding her bags, looking from her to the house.

"Sorry," she murmured, then turned away again, avoiding the driver's gaze. She took an automatic step forward but had to force the rest before he decided he'd waited long enough and set her bags down at the gate. The shadows seemed to reach for her as she passed. Ignoring them, she slid her hand into her front pocket, drawing out the keyring it had taken her the past two days to find. It held only one key, and still she fumbled as she tried to slide it into the lock.

Her bags thudded on the stoop behind her, causing her to jump. She sighed, partly in relief, partly in resignation, her shoulders hitching as the driver's steps faded back down the walk. Sheridan frowned at the difficult key only to realize her hand shook. Blinking the threat of tears from her eyes, she squared her shoulders and steadied her hand, finally sliding the key into the lock. It turned smoothly enough with a quiet *snick*.

The door swung open without a sound. The dawn's light filtering through the trees lit up the dust motes in the air past the threshold. A musty, faintly stale scent wafted out, edged with a hint of ozone. Sheridan stood there, staring into the foyer, lost in shifting shadows thicker than those dappling the yard. Or, perhaps, she only imagined it so. Her ears strained for the sounds of heartfelt greetings she feared might never come again. Not wanting to draw the neighbors' attention any more than she already had, she pivoted and took up her bags, wrestling them into the house, expecting, as always, to hear her father fussing at her to leave them for him, but hearing only silence.

Though the exterior of her childhood home remained much the same, the interior had changed beyond recognition. Stunned, Sheridan let her bags fall to the carpet as soon as she was far enough inside to close the door. She did so without turning away from the hodgepodge of wires and recording devices and tiny red-and-green sensor lights that hung on the walls like a technophile's idea of Christmas garland. None of it looked dangerous, but the implications disturbed her, increasing her sense of guilt over not coming home sooner.

"Oh, Papa..." she said aloud, her head slowly shaking from side to side. "What were you thinking?"

Again, the only response she received was silence.

Leaving her bags where they lay, Sheridan moved through the house, from the living room to the dining room and beyond, taking in the scattered piles of books and notes and the continuing strands of electrical wires. The moldering plates and filmed-over remnants of indeterminable drinks. Dust coated all things non-electrical.

She'd had no idea things had gotten this bad.

For the most part, what she could see of the furnishings remained the same but showed the same wear as the outside of the house. Still, Sheridan would have never imagined such a state. Papa had always been so particular.

Nearly without thought, Sheridan began gathering up the dishes lying about, only to stop when it became clear there were too many for her to manage, and they were not in a state worth salvaging. Instead, she went to the kitchen and dug beneath the sink until she found a box still containing garbage bags. Pulling one out, she returned to the living room to begin again. Before she could fill it, her phone rang.

Muttering a curse her parents wouldn't have approved of, Sheridan fished the cell phone out of her pocket. "Hello?"

"Ms. Cascaden?"

"Yes?"

"This is Sheriff Tompkins. We spoke a few days ago?"

Sheridan remained silent, not knowing what to say and, at the same time, afraid of the reason for this call. The sheriff cleared his throat when the silence had gone too long.

"Natty Buckalew mentioned you'd gotten into town…"

Sheridan grimaced at the mention of the across-the-street neighbor. *Once a busybody, always a busybody.* When Sheridan had been younger, the other kids had called the woman "Nosy" instead of Natty among themselves. Of course, their parents probably had too.

"Yes, sheriff, I just arrived. I'm waiting for visiting hours to head over to the hospital."

"Understood, miss, but if you wouldn't mind stopping by the Sheriff's Office on your way? We have a few questions."

"Questions?" As Sheridan straightened, her brow furrowed. "My father had a health crisis. What questions would the Sheriff's department have about that?"

"Nothing to worry about, Ms. Cascaden. It's all routine."

She noticed he hadn't answered her question.

"So, visiting hours over at Cooper General start at nine. Shall I expect you around eight? That should give us plenty of time."

Plenty of time? What the hell did he need to ask? Scowling, Sheridan glanced at the face of her phone, tapping to call up the time. Seven-thirty. Her father's car should be out back in the garage. Assuming it was in running order and charged up, eight o'clock was doable.

"That should be fine."

Without waiting for further comment, Sheridan disconnected the call and headed through the dining room, into the kitchen, aiming for the back door, only to stumble back as a ball of darkness cut across her path, low to the ground and fast. It disappeared without a sound into the sunroom off the kitchen. Her heart racing, Sheridan leaned through the doorway, eyes searching. Her father had never mentioned a cat, but she would swear that was what she'd seen. Hadn't she? There was no sign of movement. No meows or chitters or shifting of objects displaced by feline movement. Frowning, Sheridan backed into the kitchen and turned to look around. No litter box. Or smell of one. No food or water bowl. The dark blur had been too large for a mouse or other rodent intruder.

Jet lag, it has to be jet lag, she told herself, even as a fragment of memory from her childhood speared upward, of following what seemed like a dog into the bushes at school, only to have the other kids tease her for chasing shadows.

Sheridan forced the memory back. *Or maybe I'm just overwhelmed.* Who wouldn't be with their father catatonic and the local sheriff wanting to have words? She'd been going nonstop since she'd received that first phone call, the one that set all this in motion. The memories alone... then finding her childhood home in *this* state of dishevelment.

No. Now was not the time.

Shoving all her questions and concerns aside, Sheridan returned to the back door. Papa's keys sat in their usual place, a lumpy, heart-shaped "ashtray" spattered with bright yellow, red, and blue paint, the kind that came standard issue in huge squeeze bottles with every grade-school classroom. Sheridan lost her battle with her earlier tears. They slid silently down her cheeks as she reached out and ran a trembling finger over the familiar bumps of the ashtray. She had made it for Papa when she was in first grade. Never mind, he'd never smoked. He had redubbed it the "key-tray" and used that misshaped lump of clay as a catch-all since the day she'd brought it home and presented it to him.

Huffing out a breath, Sheridan grabbed up the keys and headed out back, only to reverse course, making her way through the intervening rooms to the front door, where she snatched her purse from the pile of luggage and stalked out back again, shoving all thought of her father, the past, and the current state of domestic disarray behind a huge mental slab and focusing on the point-to-point of getting to the hospital via a pit stop at the Sheriff's Office.

Behind the house stood a clapboard structure. Big for a garage, little for a barn. A legacy from when the house had been a part of a working farm, before all but the house and a quarter acre of land surrounding it had been parceled off. The bottom of the barn housed Papa's Prius, its charging station, and anything else relegated there to gather dust. Broken furniture, disused yard equipment, and the recycling he, at times, forgot to take out. The loft above, though, had always been Sheridan's refuge. Papa had converted it to a studio once she'd gone beyond the lumpy-ashtray art stage into efforts that hinted at her true passion and talent. She longed to go up there right now and lose herself in some therapeutic artwork, but she had an appointment with law enforcement. And Papa.

She opened the gate blocking the driveway, then turned to the garage. Unlocking the door and pushing it open on its sliding track, Sheridan released the smallest measure of her tension on a sigh. Papa's sea-glass green Prius sat in a carefully clear space in the center of the bay, its cable plugged into the charging station. With a heart full of misgiving for the meetings ahead, she unplugged and stowed the charging cable, then climbed behind the wheel and headed out.

Chapter Two

The town of Bradbury had changed over the past five years. More than Sheridan would have expected. That, or her memory was worth crap. Between new construction, blocked routes, and changed street names — not to mention her reason for being here in the first place — her nerves were frayed. Despite the homestead being only fifteen minutes outside of town, she pulled into the Sheriff's Office lot at quarter after eight, every muscle twitching and her teeth clenched tight enough to crack a molar. She took great care not to slam the door getting out of the car.

Still trying to compose herself, she walked into the reception area and approached the officer at the desk.

"I'm Sheridan Cascaden, here to see Sheriff Tompkins."

The young man pushed a ledger toward her. "Please sign in and have a seat. The sheriff will be with you shortly."

Sheridan swallowed the comment she wanted to make and did as he requested.

As she slid into the hard plastic chair across the room, her eyes scanned the station. Whatever transformation had hit Bradbury had missed the municipal building completely. With the — possible — exception of the staff, nothing had changed in the reception area surrounding her in at least fifteen years, not the carpet or the chairs or the tacky 20th century PSA posters. Heck, even the bitter aroma of almost-scorched coffee seemed the same.

Trying not to dwell on the last time she'd sat in these inhospitable chairs, Sheridan pulled out her phone, thinking she might as well read. Only, her earlier trembling had returned. She squeezed her eyes shut and pressed her lips together, too worn and weary to resist further as the memories slipped past her barriers.

"Sheri!" Mama said, her brow and lips drawn down as if both were pulled by a single string. Sheri watched her mother reach up and rub the wrinkles frowning made on her forehead as if trying to lay them smooth again. It didn't work. Mama sighed. "I checked your room when I tucked you in. There's nothing there." Her voice quavered, making her seem less than certain. "Please go to sleep and let me get back to work. I have piles of papers left to grade for tomorrow…"

"No! No! Please, something's watching. I can feel it! Something… mean." Sheri stood in the doorway to her parents' room, edging as close to the threshold as she dared without entering, watching Mama's face for any hint of permission. Ashamed to be so afraid, Sheri tried to stop the tremors that nearly made her teeth clack, but Mama saw them anyway.

She sighed again, looking bone-weary.

Sheri held her breath, waiting. Slowly, Mama shook her head and gave Sheri a faint smile as she patted the bed beside her. Well… actually, just a thud of her hand, like she didn't have the energy to lift it back up. The sight made Sheri feel sad and not a little guilty, but not enough that she didn't dash across the room and climb into bed beside her mother.

"You're lucky Papa is away, or it would be a pillow and blanket on the floor. Now, you lay still and go to sleep, or it's right back to your own bed."

"Yes, Mama," Sheri murmured as she snuggled down and pulled the blanket to her chin, already feeling safer. Only, she lay there, as quiet as she could, wishing she had closed the door. From the shadowy hallway, it seemed like gleaming red eyes watched her. She stared back hard enough she thought she could make out a section of deeper shadows, but solid, kind of shaped like a man, except she couldn't see any legs, just solid darkness down to the ground. This was a new one, and for the first time, a shadow felt mean and not friendly. Sheri squeezed her eyes shut only to pry them open again, too afraid to not see what was coming.

"Sheri…"

"Sorry, Mama."

The shape was gone. The red gleam was gone, like she imagined it, but it still felt like something watched.

Without her even asking, Mama got up and crossed the room. For a moment, she stood there staring out before closing the door. Sheri heard the lock click, and every muscle went limp. She waited for Mama to return to the bed, but instead, Mama slumped against the door as if to hold it closed against what lurked outside. *After a few moments, she straightened and returned, climbing into bed and taking up her grading once more.*

Sheri let out a quavering breath, then closed her eyes and tried to sleep.

She really did. But sleep wouldn't come. She lay still anyway, so still, she kind of shook just a little bit because the last thing she wanted was to be sent back to her room.

Mama must have felt her anyway. She drew a deep breath and slowly let it out. "Sit up, sweetie."

Sheri wiggled until she hit the headboard and scooched up until she was sitting pressed against her mother.

"I know it's scary sometimes, especially when it feels like someone's there you can't quite see. But they can't hurt you. They can only watch. They're like someone on the other side of a curtain, and there's no way past it."

"But I can see them, Mama... some."

Mama paled, and now she trembled. Not a lot, but she held Sheri pressed pretty close, so it was easy to feel.

"You can? Tell me. Tell me what you saw tonight."

Sheri didn't want to, not when it made Mama so frightened, even if she tried to hide it. And, more importantly, when she still had to go to sleep. She might remember him too much in her dreams. But Mama waited. "Tonight was a mean man all dark and thick, like the cutouts we did in class of our heads traced on black paper, only like he was cut out of shadow. He had on a hat with a big brim, and his eyes were kind of glowy and red. It feels like he means for me to go with him."

The trembling increased.

"He can't hurt you. He can't," *Mama murmured into Sheri's hair.* "I won't let him."

Gently, Mama set Sheri a little away from her, then reached up and pulled the necklace around her neck out of her nightgown. Mama never took it off or wore it in the open. This was the first time Sheri could remember seeing more than the chain. She stared in fascination as it rose out of the soft cotton fabric. The pendant twisted back and forth, the angled facets catching the warm light from the lamp. The design was a square with little nubs like wide, short "T"s along each side, and the center held a raised pattern made up of shapes and colors—triangles and circles and something that looked kinda like a flower. That was all Sheri saw before Mama dropped the necklace around her neck and slid the pendant inside Sheri's nightgown. When she tried to look, Mama lay her hand over it.

"Let it be, Sheridan, let it be. Keep it there, and it will keep you safe."

"What is it?"

"Some would call it a yantra, but I know it by a different name."

"What's that?"

It seemed like Mama fought with herself if she would speak the word. In the end, she shook her head.

"It doesn't matter. Yantra serves well enough. This one is special, different," Mama said with the weariest of smiles like her energy was all spent. "Think of it like a shield. A wall behind the curtain. It will keep you safe right in here so that no one can pull you away somewhere else."

"Pull me away?"

"Don't you worry. Just don't ever take it off. Promise."

Capturing her lower lip between her teeth, Sheri glanced at the door and then up at Mama.

"What about you? What's gonna keep you safe now?"

Mama flinched, then forced a smile. "I'm not the one seeing mean shadows, am I?"

Sheri nodded, but she continued to tremble.

"I wish Papa was coming home tonight," she murmured.

"Me too," Mama sighed, then she glanced at her grading. "I'll wake up early and finish in the morning. Now lay down. It's time to sleep."

Sheri scooched back down until Papa's pillow cradled her head. Mama smiled at her, then leaned over to press a kiss on her forehead. "I love you, Sheri-Berry."

"I love you, Mama-Berry."

Chuckling, Mama clicked off the light and slid down into the bed, curling herself around Sheri. With her mother's lips pressed again to her head and the sound of her humming acting as a lullaby, Sheri drifted off.

She woke much later, with a gasp trapped on her lips. The malevolence had returned, a solid blanket of darkness smothering the room. Though she knew Mama lay right beside her, Sheri couldn't feel or hear her. The malevolence, however, had moved, a solid presence just inside the door. In her head, Sheri screamed and screamed and screamed though only she could hear it as a shape of pure evil separated from the surrounding darkness to lean over the bed, broken only by the smolder of two red glowing points under what seemed like a wide brim.

Sheri fought to move. To cry out. But as the figure leaned closer, all Sheri could do was gape. Something seemed off. Like she was merely an observer. Though she was not the object of the watcher's gaze, she felt it like a tangible weight pressing her into the mattress. If she could have squeezed her eyes shut, she would have. Silently, Sheri cried out for her mother as the figure moved beside her to where Mama lay.

After what seemed like forever, microtremors shook Sheri's body, breaking the grip of whatever had held her still as the faintest touch of moonlight seeped back into the room. She jerked upright at the sudden sound of her own screams, alone in her parents' bed, with scattered papers drifting like white ghosts to the floor and glowing scarlet eyes narrowing beneath their hat brim as the shadow seemed to slide through the wall...

...Sheridan jerked back with a gasp, looking up to discover the silhouette of a man in a broad-brimmed hat leaning over her, an echo of the last time she'd ever seen her mother. She scrambled up and to her left, the sound of her chair toppling into the others no more than a faint clatter in her ringing ears. Her gaze never left the man before her.

"Whoa! Whoa! Hey, now... take it easy there, Ms. Cascaden."

She blinked, a rapid flutter as she fought to bring her breathing under control, wanting to sink into the floor as everyone in the reception area of the Bradbury Sheriff's Office watched the lunatic knocking over chairs. Sheriff Tompkins himself, presumably, stood before her, his expression a mix of perplexed and concerned. "You okay?"

Sheridan felt herself go flush and dropped her gaze, rubbing at her head where her temple had begun to throb. How could she answer? The rogue memory had left her shaken, disoriented. She raised a hand to her bare neck, worry gnawing at her. Where had the pendant gone? Where had Mama gone? As a child, she'd blocked out the memories of her mother's disappearance. There had been brief flashes over the years, but nothing this vivid or detailed. She shook her head to clear it, not in response.

"I am so sorry, sheriff..."

"No worries... How about you and I go back to my office where we can speak in private?" At Sheridan's nod, he guided her with the barest touch on the back of her arm toward the hallway past reception, where a cluster of office staff scattered back to their respective duties. As Sheridan and her escort passed the desk, Sheriff Tompkins paused a moment and addressed the officer on duty. "Jeffries, please have Andrews bring back some tea for Ms. Cascaden, or" —he turned to Sheridan— "sorry, is there something else you rather have to settle you?"

She really, *really* wanted to say a whiskey but resisted the urge. "Thank you, tea is fine."

With a nod, the sheriff led her down the hallway and into his office.

"Please, have a seat, miss." As he removed his hat and hung it on a peg on the back of the door, Sheriff Tompkins gestured toward a chair the cousin to the one outside. "Do you mind if I close the door?"

Sheridan pivoted toward Tompkins halfway to the seat. "What is this about, sheriff?"

"Just some routine questions, Ms. Cascaden." The sheriff's tone remained neutral. "I figured you might be more comfortable with a measure of privacy."

"I'm not sure what your definition of routine is, sheriff, but you have managed to make me less comfortable, not more."

"Please…" Tompkins gestured again toward the seat as a young man in a deputy's uniform entered the room with care, balancing a precarious tray crammed with three teacups and what seemed like every possible option of creamer and sweetener and snack to be had.

The tag on his uniform read *Deputy Andrews*.

Sheridan's eyes widened before a smile tugged the corners of her lips. The sight of the deputy warmed her heart. Apparently, Bradbury and its people had changed in more progressive ways than she'd realized. The population as a whole had not been very accepting of those who were different when she'd been growing up, as she should know. But Andrews had the features of an individual born with Down syndrome. Stocky but fit and a touch awkward, he moved with extreme care. He did grow flustered, however, when he approached the desk and there was nowhere clear to set his burden down. The sheriff moved forward and accepted the tray.

"Thank you, Andrews," he said with a patient smile.

"I didn't know what she likes, so I brought some of everything."

"You did good, Andrews. Could you please see if Jeffries needs anything?"

At the sheriff's praise, Andrews grinned, pleasure lighting up his face. He straightened and incongruously saluted Tompkins before waving at Sheridan, then hurrying out the door on his mission.

Sheridan's smile widened as she waved back, then turned toward the sheriff.

"Please, Ms. Cascaden, sit down."

"Is he truly a deputy?"

Clearly misunderstanding, Tompkins' expression took on a touch of disapproval as he set down the tray on top of a stack of folders. "Without any doubt. Deputy Andrews is a valued member of the sheriff's department and has sworn an oath to serve this community. He is one of my most diligent support staff."

"I'm very glad to hear that," she said, her words relaxed and warm, not rising to the censure in his voice. "Everyone deserves a place where they can feel useful and engaged, no matter the challenges they face."

Sheriff Tompkins looked thrown by her response but nodded. "If we could return to the matter at hand?"

"Of course." Sheridan sat and waited for the sheriff's first question.

He sighed and dropped his head a moment before catching her eye and gesturing to the tray. "The tea, Ms. Cascaden."

"Sorry..." As he waved off her apology, Sheridan sat forward and claimed a steaming cup of what turned out to be Lady Grey and doctored it with a healthy dollop of honey before also selecting a slightly damp donut from the tray. The sheriff waited for her to finish her refreshments before taking out a recording device and starting in on his questions.

"When was the last time you saw your father?"

"Several months ago, he flew into Denver for a visit."

"Did you notice anything different about him? Anything off?"

"No."

"Does your father have a history of substance abuse?"

Sheridan jarred back as if slapped. "Excuse me?"

"Does your father have a history of substance abuse?"

"No! Why would you even ask such a thing?"

"Have you noticed any changes in his behavior since his visit? Distraction or uncharacteristic reactions during phone conversations? Nonsensical responses?"

Sheridan flashed back to when she'd walked into the house this morning. Her shock at the state of things. So unexpected. Troubling, even. A sign Papa had lost himself in his work? Or an indication he'd lost himself altogether? Cutting off that line of thought, Sheridan met the sheriff's gaze and firmed her jaw. She could not, *would* not believe that of her father, not without more evidence than supposition. With great care, she set her empty teacup on the sheriff's desk and leaned toward him. "I said, why would you even ask such a thing?"

"Please answer the question, Ms. Cascaden."

"My father has had a stroke!"

Something shifted in the sheriff's expression, not quite a wince but akin to one. "There have been recent reports of your father behaving erratically, and this" — the sheriff held up a folder with her father's name on it — "this toxicology report shows traces of a controlled substance in his system. He was discovered in the foothills after midnight, with no indication of how he got there. Either he acted in a manner that had adverse consequences, or someone else did this to him. It is my job to rule out those potential scenarios. Now please answer the question."

At the mention of foul play, Sheridan stiffened, her mind racing to consider the potential explanation that had not until now occurred to her. She locked down the impulse to shudder.

"Ms. Cascaden…"

"No!"

"Is that your answer or your refusal?"

Sheridan gritted her teeth, having no answer to give. "It is after nine a.m., sheriff. I need to go check on my father. Unless I am for some reason being detained?"

Sheriff Tompkins frowned. "Of course not."

Without bidding him good day or anything else, Sheridan stood and hurried from the room, not trusting herself to speak another word.

Chapter Three

Cooper General was a lot easier to find than the Sheriff's Office. Not any easier to get into, though. Even here, subtle changes and ongoing updates and construction had Sheridan all turned around, but eventually, she found her way to Reception.

"…You want to turn down this hallway on the right, but don't take these elevators. They're under maintenance. Keep going to the next left and take the stairwell right there to the second floor, then…"

Sheridan's right eye twitched as the receptionist gave her even more convoluted directions on how to get to her father's room. Right now, all she wanted to do was crawl into an empty bed somewhere and tell herself this was all a bad dream. She'd barely had any sleep since receiving the call telling her Papa was in the hospital. And after the long flight here and all that had already happened that day, Sheridan was done in, and it wasn't even noon.

Somehow, she made it to the correct room.

Standing outside the doorway, Sheridan watched a nurse bustle about inside, adjusting an IV and checking vitals before initialing the whiteboard in the corner and hurrying out the door. All the while, Papa lay there unmoving, his body as wrapped in wires, it seemed, as his home was. Oddly, his face stood out almost a healthy pink against the whites and beiges of the room, the bright lights above chasing away any shadows.

Sheridan found the machines he was plugged into almost soothing in their regular rhythms. And the air was surprisingly neutral. Not at all what she'd expected.

Yet she couldn't bring herself to enter.

Stepping into that room made the risk all too real.

"Excuse me," someone spoke beside her. "Are you Mr. Cascaden's family?"

Slowly, Sheridan turned to look at the doctor waiting beside her. He looked a bit young, but as his calm confidence brushed against her, the tension building all morning relaxed a bit, and the throb at her temple settled down into a dull ache. She nearly cried in relief but managed to hold back.

She nodded. "Sheridan Cascaden, his daughter."

"I am Dr. Varughese. I am overseeing your father's care."

Sheridan accepted the hand he extended. "What can you tell me about his condition?"

"Please…" Dr. Varughese gestured toward her father's room. "Shall we step inside?"

Feeling odd talking about her father while he lay right there, Sheridan checked to see that the other bed in the room was empty before moving to the far side by the window. She leaned against the sill and waited for the doctor to begin.

Dr. Varughese's pleasant, neutral expression flattened into an almost grimace. He looked down at his hands a moment before meeting her gaze once more. "I'm sorry, Ms. Cascaden, there isn't a lot I can tell you. There is no sign of… trauma. At first, we believed he might have had a stroke or perhaps the start of an aneurism, but neither proved to be the case. Nothing in his health profile explains the situation. At the moment, he is stable but unresponsive."

"So, he's in a coma?"

"Precisely, but we can't identify the cause."

Thinking of her earlier conversation with the sheriff, Sheridan caught the inside of her lip between her teeth and debated the wisdom of her next question.

"Sheriff Tompkins said there were signs of controlled substances in my father's bloodwork."

Dr. Varughese slipped briefly into a full grimace and shook his head. Sheridan had the sense what she'd said annoyed him, though his professionalism reasserted itself. "As convenient an explanation as that might be, there were only trace readings. *Trace*. Nothing to suggest substance abuse and no physical evidence of drug use. For all we know, he could have eaten a poppy seed bagel or something else that skewed the results."

Sheridan found some reassurance in his words. "Thank you. If there isn't anything else, I'd like to see my father."

With a nod, the doctor stepped to the side, his arm gesturing her forward. As Sheridan moved to stand by Papa's bed, the doctor proceeded to leave, but something bothered her.

"Dr. Varughese?"

He stopped and turned in the doorway. "Yes?"

"When we were speaking, you seemed to hesitate when you said there were no signs of trauma. Why?"

The good doctor drew a deep breath, and his lips slightly quirked as if he rather not verbalize the cause of his hesitation.

"*Why?*" she persisted.

"As I said, there were no signs of trauma... but if you look on his right arm, you'll find black marks that we cannot explain. They aren't bruises, and they don't appear to be ink or paint. The skin is just... black. We have no way of knowing how long they've been there, but it seems notable."

Sheridan felt her brow furrow and the corners of her mouth draw down slightly, only realizing as he turned to leave that the doctor wore much the same expression. Clearly, neither of them knew what to make of the information. Releasing a sigh, Sheridan slipped into the chair beside her father's bed. She reached out and drew the blanket down. For a moment, her breath caught in her chest as she saw what the doctor had described. If not for the odd spacing and drawn-out look to them, like smudged charcoal, Sheridan would almost say the black marks on her father's arm had the look of gripping fingers.

Idly, she rubbed her left wrist where a tribal-style tattoo covered similar markings for the most part. Shivering, she pulled the covers over her father and held his hand through the thin blanket.

All through visiting hours, she sat there, sometimes silent, sometimes reminiscing, but always conscious that his... essence... wandered elsewhere. As cliché as it sounded, not like he wasn't paying attention, but rather no one was home.

She almost didn't notice when the alert announcing the end of visiting hours played over the hospital speakers in the hallway. A nurse popped her head in the door to remind her. Fighting tears once more, Sheridan stood and leaned over the bedrail, brushing back her father's hair from his forehead and placing a gentle kiss there instead.

"I miss you, Papa," she murmured. "Please come back to me."

Chapter Four

As she left her father's room, Sheridan came within inches of slamming into one of the nurses. She stopped abruptly and nearly lost her balance.

The woman reached out to catch her.

"Oh, my! I am so sorry…" Sheridan said, looking down at the nurse's nametag: *K. McAllister, LPN*. Her brow furrowed at the name as she looked up to take in the nurse's face and her honey-blonde hair, done up in a French twist. Sheridan found faint traces of the familiar there. "K-Katie?"

"It's Kate," the woman answered, her tone flat and her shoulders going stiff as she likewise cataloged Sheridan's features and her eyes flickered to the name written beside the patient's door. "Good to see you, Sheri…"

"Sheridan," she murmured.

"…sorry to hear about your father, but I need to finish my rounds," Kate continued as if Sheridan hadn't spoken.

"Of course." She stepped to the side as her one-time friend blew her off as she had many times before, if long ago. It hurt just as much now. As the memories surfaced again, Sheridan hurried to leave the hospital before they overwhelmed her.

Alone, as always, Sheridan sat across the playground from the other sixth graders, pushing herself on the wonky swing no one ever wanted a turn on. She didn't mind. Better to be alone and watch the fun than surrounded by the others and being the "fun."

The popular kids thought she was a weirdo freak. Most of the others did too.

She tried not to supply them with any more proof. Not because she cared what they thought or what they would do, but because it wasn't worth the endless visits to the school psychologist. Or Papa's disappointment when he got another call from the principal.

Except that today, she wasn't sure she had a choice.

Not too far away stood the jungle gym. One of those sturdy industrial ones, made from two thick, arched metal poles with thinner bars welded to each one connecting them along the length, like a ladder doing a backbend. The boys always swung from the bars like monkeys or action heroes, but the girls liked to stand on top and pretend to be circus performers. Sheridan watched as Katie McAllister scaled the rungs. When Sheridan turned her head and looked away, from the corner of her eye, she spied more shadows moving beneath Katie than there should have been. When Sheridan glanced back, they flickered away, vanishing as if behind a wall, but she caught their jerky movement before they were gone, shadowy hands reaching out to pluck at Katie's feet.

Dread roiled within Sheridan until she felt sick to her stomach.

You would think she would learn. Remember that she was different than pretty much everyone she knew and keep quiet about the things she saw... the things she sensed. It wasn't like the Watchers could do anything, right? At least not that she had ever seen. But Sheridan could feel that some of them had evil intent, even if they couldn't follow through. But every once in a while — like today — they tried, just in case.

What if Sheridan kept quiet, and someday they succeeded?

Would Katie pay for Sheridan's silence? Or someone else like her?

Still, the shadows had never done anything. Had they? They'd just... been there, right?

A tiny whisp of nearly remembered fear twined along Sheridan's spine and then was gone. Shaking it off, she thought of the good times when some of the shadows had played with her back when she was younger, at times her only friends. Well, played as much as anyone could without being able to talk or touch. Peek-a-boo as a toddler had transitioned into hide-and-seek and complex, ongoing rounds of what she liked to call 'Where's Shadow.' But this was nothing as harmless as that.

She struggled with her doubts. What difference could the rantings of a crazy kid make?

Sheridan was about to find out.

Dragging her feet over the ground to stop her swing from swaying, Sheridan stood and walked over to the jungle gym.

"Hi, Katie."

"Hey, Sheri!"

Sheridan frowned. She hadn't been called Sheri since her mother disappeared, and she preferred it that way. But it felt like she and Katie were starting to become friends, so Sheridan remained silent on the matter.

Katie lowered herself to the bars, looping her legs through and dangling down until they were face to face, her long blonde hair all but brushed the ground. Sheridan grinned, but her gaze darted around the playground, trying to catch shadows out of the corner of her eyes. Katie grinned back but gave her an odd look like she was trying to figure Sheridan out.

Good luck with that!

"What's up?" Katie asked, gripping the bars over her head and dropping her legs to the ground before turning around until they faced one another. Sheridan relaxed a bit once Katie no longer dangled, but just a little, still feeling driven to speak.

"You know… sometimes…" Sheridan hesitated, every instinct screaming at her not to say the words but unable to help herself. Too worried about what could happen to this girl who had always been kind to her, who almost felt like she could be a friend. "Sometimes, there are people there, and we can't quite see them."

Katie crinkled her nose and tilted her head like she was trying to decide if Sheridan was serious, but, in the end, Katie laughed like Sheridan was being funny.

Sheridan did not laugh with her.

Katie stopped, the carefree sound trailing off into awkwardness. "You're kidding, right?"

"Haven't you ever felt it?" Sheridan asked. "A faint chill across your skin, like a brush of air passing, with nothing to disturb it? The sensation that someone is there? That someone is watching you, but you can't see them? Or the shadows kinda look a little… thicker? Or you see a flutter of movement out of the corner of your eye, and when you turn, there's nothing there? I've seen them. They follow us sometimes, watching, and not all of them are good."

All hint of her laughter vanished, and Kate shifted sideways, her movements tense, awkward, as she tried to edge away without seeming she was edging away.

"Um, I forgot… Ms. Lachewitz wants to see me," she mumbled as she not-quite smiled and moved off. Sheridan's stomach clenched, and she put on a smile as fake as Katie's as she watched her hurry away.

Shaking off the heartache of years past, Sheridan realized there was a good reason she'd never returned to Bradbury once she'd gotten out. And yet, at the moment, home was her only refuge. With a sigh, she climbed into her father's Prius. First, she swung by the market to get some supplies—including enough paper plates and cups to hold her until she could replace the things she'd tossed—and then headed for the outskirts of town.

Chapter Five

And so, Sheridan's life went day by day, night by night, for the next few days. During visiting hours, she parked her butt beside her father's bed. She read to him or talked to him and even helped with his massage therapy. So far, to little effect.

Outside of visiting hours, she parked her butt at the dining room table, sorting like an urban archeologist through the layers and mounds accumulated there. Here, she made more progress. The situation had gone from barely contained chaos to orderly piles of organized materials. One for physical/mental conditions, one for strange phenomena, and one for everything else. The tabletop remained covered but at least manageable, nothing threatening to cascade to the floor, anyway.

She could not make much sense of any of the papers or even her father's notes—yet. But she figured it was better to first inflict order on the situation and then wrestle with understanding.

Once the dining room had been pacified, she'd gone through the rest of the house—except for the study—migrating anything that looked related or important to the appropriate, centrally-located pile.

Her childhood home very nearly looked respectable again.

Oh, *fine*.

Her childhood home no longer looked like a hoarder starter kit.

She felt much better about the situation after that.

And then her phone rang.

The screen displayed the word "Restricted" above an unfamiliar number.

Sheridan picked it up, her stomach turning squirrelly in an instant.

"Hello?"

"Ms. Cascaden, this is Dr. Varughese. Are you at home?"

Her stomach dropped. "I am. What's wrong?"

"Your father has had a minor stroke. We have him stabilized, but I think you should come down."

If the good doctor said anything else, Sheridan missed it. She'd already hung up, grabbing her purse from the kitchen counter and the keys from the key-tray on her way out the door. Afraid something like this might happen, she'd taken to keeping the car fully charged and in the driveway at all times. She slid open the gate and climbed into the car, on her way in less than five minutes. In less than ten, she reached the hospital, expecting the sheriff's department to pull her over at any second.

Dr. Varughese met her at reception.

Sheridan stopped at the sight of him, a cold wave sluicing down her body.

He made a soothing sound as he came up to her, a gentle smile on his face. "No, no, nothing has changed." With a brief touch on her arm, he gestured with his other hand toward a sign that read *Cafeteria*. "Come, have a cup of coffee with me."

Shaking her head, Sheridan pulled back. "I have to see my father."

Dr. Varughese nodded. "You will. Right now, everything is fine. I have just seen him, and his vitals are good. It was a small stroke, so small we never would have been aware of it if he weren't being monitored.

"Please, let's go where we can talk in more comfort."

She caught her bottom lip between her teeth and struggled with what to do. What if the doctor was wrong? What if something happened and she wasn't there?

Varughese waited patiently, encouraging her with his eyes and a light but steady pressure on her arm. "We won't be long." Then he held up his pager and waggled it at her. "And we are only a buzz away from hurrying back if need be."

Accepting that he would not relent, Sheridan let herself be guided. They both remained silent as they traveled down a corridor unfamiliar to Sheridan, past more renovations, to an elevator that looked like it dated back to the founding of the town and the original raising of the building. Dr. Varughese held the door while she stepped inside, then he followed, pulling an actual accordion gate across the opening before taking them down to the next floor with a lever, no buttons in sight.

She looked at him in shock as they came to a stop and reversed the process to exit.

He chuckled and pointed at the historical society plaque on the wall outside the elevator. "They keep it for the charm... and the extra funding."

Sheridan just nodded and followed him down the brightly lit hall toward glass double doors decorated with painted murals of smiling sandwiches and cheery muffins surrounded by colorful flowers. Dr. Varughese handed her a tray and guided her toward the self-serve line. When he realized she followed him without selecting anything, he slid a slice of cling-wrapped pie onto her tray, followed by an insulated cup filled three-quarters of the way with coffee. "Sugar and cream are right over there."

She glanced at the tray, then up at him. "Rather presumptuous, don't you think?"

He leveled a knowing look back. "You are pale and shocky, as demonstrated by your slowed response and the lack of focus in your gaze. This will not be an easy conversation. You will need the sugar and caffeine to aid your concentration. Doctor's orders. Besides, I've already paid."

Frowning, she dutifully went to the condiment station and finished off the coffee with three packets of sugar and a generous pour of cream before following the doctor to a corner table out of the way of the few late-night patrons. As they settled in, he handed her a plastic fork and waited for her to unwrap her pie. She humored him, mostly because it was doubtful he would begin until she followed orders.

She found the cherry pie surprisingly good, both sweet and tart, with a buttery, flaky crust. The coffee—as she'd expected—was hot creamy tar. Her grimace betrayed her. The doc chuckled and handed her a fourth packet of sugar.

"Sorry. They make it 24-hour-shift strong around here."

Sheridan grumbled and finished her pie, only sipping at the re-doctored coffee. Dr. Varughese merely warmed his hands on his cup, chatting about the renovations disrupting the hospital and the various items the cafeteria served that should be either avoided or sought out.

As she pushed her tray away and sat back, the doctor looked down at the table, then back up again, his head tilted slightly to the side as if bracing himself for the unpleasant.

"Your father has had what is called a transient ischemic attack, also called a ministroke. It has all of the same symptoms as a full stroke, but the side effects generally resolve in a matter of hours.

"Unfortunately, this type of occurrence can be a precursor to a more major event."

He paused as if waiting for a response. Finding it difficult to breathe, let alone talk, Sheridan took a gulp of her neglected coffee and nodded.

Dr. Varughese watched her closely, his brow furrowed. "Our concern is that this is a sign of his body breaking down. That whatever caused his coma is not something he will recover from."

Sheridan felt a tremor go through her, clenching her muscles tight. "What are you getting at, doctor?"

"Does your father have a Living Will?"

The pie and coffee she'd consumed threatened to reverse the process.

"I-I don't know."

She didn't realize until the doctor reached out to lay his hand over hers that she continued to shake. "You must prepare yourself, Ms. Cascaden. Right now, there is virtually no brain activity. While it is not unheard of for patients in this condition to recover, it is highly unlikely. At some point, you'll need to decide when enough is enough. Many more events like today, and his body will no longer be able to sustain him unaided. Should the worst occur, the decision could well be made for you."

Sheridan felt a ripple roll through her stomach, edging toward her throat. She pushed to her feet and shoved her chair back in one jerky move, stumbling away, frantically searching for the sign pointing to the restroom. She barely made it in time. As she tried to rinse the taste of sick from her mouth, the door squeaked open. Lifting her head, she glanced in the mirror rather than turning around. Mortified, she met Kate's gaze. Her one-time friend looked almost sympathetic.

"Dr. Varughese asked me to check on you."

Sheridan looked away, turning the spigot back on to splash some cool water on her face. "I'm fine, thank you. I'll be right out."

Kate nodded and turned away, only to stop with her hand raised to the door. She didn't turn around but glanced over her shoulder. "I really am sorry about your father. If there's anything I can do…"

With a smile that looked more like a grimace, Sheridan nodded. "Thank you."

Once Kate left, Sheridan took a few moments to make sure she'd cleaned everything up before following her one-time—sometime?—friend out the door.

Dr. Varughese waited for her. Sheridan barely remembered following him upstairs to her father's room. Still, she would never forget how Papa looked, wan and somehow smaller than yesterday, with even more wires and tubes trailing away from him.

Dr. Varughese's words echoed in her thoughts. *You have to prepare yourself...*

Somehow, Sheridan got home, once more expecting the sheriff's department to pull her over any moment. The last thing she remembered was crawling into her father's bed.

Chapter Six

Sheridan woke with a scream trapped behind her lips. A heavy weight seemed to press down upon her, pinning her in place beneath the blankets. For an endless moment, she could not move except for her eyes and a faint twitching of her fingertips. Cold sweat pooled beneath her body as her eyes darted from point to point, searching the dark spaces of her father's room, those places untouched by the faint moonlight coming through the window.

This time she spied nothing. *This time...*

...Any time? It had been so long since she'd had an episode like this. Not since... not since she'd last lived in this house. She told herself it was the stress of the situation. And yet... a lingering essence of malevolence flavored each strangled breath she drew.

With a spasm, her muscles unclenched, and she jerked upright, gasping. As the arrested scream escaped, her body shook. She stared at her reflection in the mirror across from the bed and, for a brief instant, saw a mere silhouette, a deep, inky black shape with a pale blue-white glimmer where her eyes should be. She squeezed her eyes shut and shook her head before opening them again to meet her reflection, now as it should be, though the moonlight streaming through the window had not changed. She ran a trembling hand over a face as pale as those moonbeams, wiping away a clinging film of sour sweat as she pushed back tangled tendrils of hair the shade of deepest, darkest crimson, like heart's blood spilling across her shoulders.

On the far side of the room, pinpoints of light flashed red before subsiding back to green, then going dark, indicating the sensors positioned on every surface—perhaps even inserted into the mattress beneath her—had captured the episode before falling dormant once more. Her shoulders knotted and hunched as she envisioned some printer in the room across the hall mindlessly generating reports. *How much undissected data filled her father's dusty hard drive? How many automatic printouts littered the floor?*

A grimace stretched the taut muscles of Sheridan's face.

Why am I even still here? She shied from the thought, not quite knowing herself how she meant that or how she would answer. Not for the first time, part of her wondered if this was evidence of pending madness taking hold. Papa would have drawn her close and shooed those fears away, telling her just because a thing was unexplained didn't mean it wasn't real.

Only Papa was gone, or near enough. And from the evidence surrounding her, she had to admit he might not have been completely sane.

The thought felt like a betrayal.

Tugging at the blankets, Sheridan drew them up her shoulders and over her head. The edges she twined about her limbs and her limbs about her body. Only her face was left uncovered, draped in the curtain of her hair. She drew the blanket the rest of the way closed and sat there, swaddled.

Her ears strained, listening.

"Sher...?" Her name whispered across raw nerves, though silence hung heavy around her. Immediately, her eyes and teeth clenched at the bittersweet memory of her father's voice. She tensed until the huddle she'd curled into drew even tighter. Her sense of feeling watched intensified, though the door remained closed. The sensors dark. The house empty save for her.

"Honey, what's wrong?"

Or so she tried to reassure herself.

"Sheridan, are you okay?"

No. No, she was not okay! And it was unfair for anyone to expect her to be, figment or not. She'd been told she had to choose between letting her father waste away and cutting the cord to his survival. What loving daughter would be okay with that? And then to return here, all alone with her ghosts. Her nightmares. Her fears. A shadow living in a world of light.

How she longed to hear Papa's voice in truth. After her disturbing conversation with Dr. Varughese, then seeing Papa in that hospital bed, more faded than before, she had given in to the impulse to sleep in his room, to feel like the real him — the one she remembered — was nearby.

And look what it had gotten her. Another "episode," as Papa had called them. Worse than any she had ever had before she'd left home. She had almost forgotten what they were like. It had been so long.

Sheridan swallowed hard, trying to clear her tightening throat. She swiped her lips with her tongue, but to little effect. Her mouth was equally as dry. A part of her felt lost without him. Though they had lived apart until recently, they had spoken at least once a week.

While she was quite capable and self-sufficient, she had never fit into what her father would have called societal norms, even when the episodes were on hiatus. She and *Aunt* Bonnie—the distant cousin she had been sent to live with—hadn't lasted long. A year at most, bumping heads and locking horns all the way. Without Papa, Sheridan would truly be all alone.

"Just a bad dream, Papa," she murmured to a memory, her voice muffled within her makeshift womb.

Her lie was met by silence, and she drew herself tighter, listening to her heartbeat, dreaming she heard… no, that wasn't quite right… *felt* beneath that pulsing a deeper echo. She let herself pretend it was her mother, still wrapped around her, and that horrible night long ago had never happened. That she wasn't alone now with no one left to stand between her and the darkness.

Sighing, Sheridan forced herself from her fetal cocoon and lay back down for sleep. This had to end. She either needed to find out what happened to her father or be forced to lay him to rest. The very thought sent fresh tremors through her body.

"*Sher…?*" Again, the past echoed her name into the silence.

"Good night, Papa," she murmured as sleep reclaimed her.

Chapter Seven

Bright sunbeams streamed across the foot of Sheridan's bed while lingering warmth wrapped her like a hug, slowly fading as she blinked away sleep. Before she came completely awake, she would almost swear she felt a faint pressure across her toes, like the brush of a hand. Her sleepy, hopeful brain told her it was Papa, waking her as he had done many times before, gently so as not to startle her.

Sheridan's lips curled into a smile, but when her eyes fluttered open, all she spied was the warm glow of dust motes dancing in the sunshine. For a moment, something larger and brighter seemed to flicker in the corner of her eye, but when she rolled her head to the side, she saw nothing there.

"Oh, Papa," she murmured aloud. "What the hell's going on? What happened to you?"

Despite her concern, and the episode the night before, she felt almost rested with a sense of well-being she couldn't explain, the terror fading with dawn's light. She lay there and reached above her head in a slow stretch. Her gaze traveled around the room, taking comfort in the familiar setting of her parents' room. A well-used dresser with a full-sized mirror—old but hardly what she would call an antique—sat beneath the high window at the foot of the bed. A matching chest of drawers anchored the wall to the right of the double bed, between the closet and the door. The bed itself rested against the facing wall, with a nightstand beside it, also to the right.

Normal bedroom décor, save that across the tops of all of them ran a maze of wires and electronics. The same with the walls, studded with sensors and cameras and such to the point that every angle of the room was recorded in one manner or another. More evidence of her father's fixation. Sheridan had had no idea things had gotten this bad. Her father always sounded quite reasonable on the phone and seemed perfectly normal whenever he visited. This spoke of whole new levels of obsession.

Like herself, Papa suffered from night terrors, or so various doctors diagnosed over the years, with minor variations on the particulars. He had been obsessed with figuring out why, immersing himself in research and theory, even pop culture and urban legend. Not wanting to make herself more of an oddball than she already was, Sheridan had focused on art and left him to do his own thing.

Her father set more store in his own research than he did in the doctors. Sheridan didn't know why. He had told her once, though, that *"nothing of substance was ever gained by going with the easy answer, and Occam, be damned."* She hadn't fully understood him then, being all of ten and not exactly conversant with philosophy. As she grew older, she had to agree, though mostly because, in her experience, life seldom *gave* easy answers.

Anyway, Papa had spent her entire life trying to prove at least one of his theories. Until she'd returned home, she hadn't realized he'd been using himself as a test subject. She had no idea what, if any, progress he had made. He had always resisted her involvement. Of course, Sheridan supposed she had now inadvertently contributed to the study, whether he liked it or not, presuming he ever returned. A shiver skated down her spine, clenching her gut and rippling outward until goosebumps prickled her flesh.

Throwing aside the thought, along with the blankets, she swung her legs to the floor and returned to her old room—where she'd left her bags—to prepare for the day. She had planned to head back to the hospital that morning for another visit and then perhaps knock around town to see if anyone had any idea what had happened to her father. Instead, she pulled on an old tee shirt and a pair of sweats so paint-spattered the original color was lost to history. She didn't bother with breakfast, or even shoes, just sliding on a pair of crocs as she went out the back door.

Long ago, well before she'd struck out on her own, Papa had converted the loft apartment over the garage into an art studio. Ever since, it had been her refuge, art—of any kind—being the only therapy she had ever embraced. She had work hung in a few galleries back in Denver and had achieved some local acclaim, but the appellation "starving artist" would have all too likely applied if not for her day job teaching art basics to pre-teens and retirees in the local community. Art, though... it sustained her, grounded her.

Now was no exception. Sheridan let herself into the garage-cum-workshop and climbed the internal stairs, any remaining vestiges of tension from the night before draining away with each step upward. Here, she had everything she could possibly need to purge her demons, be it through painting, sculpture, photography, or any other medium.

Today, her fingers itched and twitched for a thick stick of graphite and a creamy white page. Ignoring the interior corner holding her sculpting supplies and kiln, Sheridan moved toward the far corner where a drafting table and several covered easels stood waiting, like soldiers at parade rest, facing a bank of windows that stretched floor to ceiling, bathing them in a warm glow of natural light.

With care, she uncovered one of the easels and unclipped an unfinished piece she'd long forgotten. Even so, she turned and slid it into a nearby art drawer for protection, then clipped a clean sheet of Strathmore Charcoal Paper in its place. Standing before the easel, she closed her eyes and let the night's demons rise. Picking up a fresh graphite stick from several still waiting on the easel ledge, she captured the previous night's episode on the page in broad, deep strokes, not guiding her hand but letting it flow. Hard angles and sharp lines trailed off into chaotic swirls. The impression of a broad-brimmed hat, a hint of a chiseled jaw, the rest fading into an amorphous form. On impulse, she set down the graphite and picked up a crimson color stick. With a few sharp twists of her wrist, the center of two eye-like swirls took on a sullen red glow. She shuddered at the effect.

Just right. *Too* right.

She looked away, sorting through the supplies at the ready on the easel's ledge for a tortillion, using the layered and tapered paper to soften and blur selective edges, robbing them of their power and trapping the essence of her night terror on the page.

As she worked, gradients of grey and black dominated the piece, as was to be expected... all save in one upper corner that she had left untouched, where a small circular portion of negative space took on the aspect of radiance floating above the darkness. Setting down the blending tool, she reached for a white pencil without looking away, fascinated by the unexpected contrast. With a few subtle strokes, she accentuated the effect. Setting the white pencil aside, she then grasped the blender once more, only to put it down again and step back from the easel.

Without the weight of her tools to anchor it, her hand shook, the faint trembling telling her more than anything else that she'd lost herself in the piece. Or maybe that she should have eaten before coming up to the loft. She glanced toward the clock above the stairwell, unsurprised to see that noon had come and gone several hours ago.

Her gaze trailed back to her newest creation. The play of light against the shadow felt like a battle between hope and hell. A frenetic image, but it brought her peace.

Most times, she didn't bother preserving reactive sketches like this one. Her art drawers would be full to overflowing. But something about the piece spoke to her. Slowly, she moved toward the storage crates beneath the nearby window, sorting through them until she found a can of fixative. Grabbing a respirator from the same crate, she put it on, then opened the window in front of her before moving back to stand before the easel. With quick even strokes, she sprayed her morning's work and left it to dry as she returned to the house in search of food.

As she exited the garage, she slowed, then stopped, her eyes drifting closed as she lifted her face to the sun's warmth. Back home—or where she paid rent, anyway—she rarely had time to stop and enjoy the pleasures of nature. Her chest rose and fell in deep, measured breaths as she basked in the moment, the soft spring breeze tugging at her crimson locks. The jasmine and clematis blooming in the front yard perfumed the air, soothing her further.

Sheridan lost herself a while in the peaceful respite.

Chapter Eight

Sheridan had no idea how much time had passed when the sudden sound of footsteps and a man clearing his throat shattered her trance. Her eyes snapped open as a sharp current of tension coursed through her body. A dark silhouette loomed over her, limned by the sun. She flinched back, her body shifting into a more stable stance, her hands coming up in defense.

"So sorry," the man murmured, the papers he held rustling as he shifted further away from her. She could see his features now, but he was still a stranger to her. Except for his bright blue eyes, though she couldn't say why. "Didn't mean to startle you. I was looking for Richard…"

Sheridan blinked, confused until she realized he meant Papa. "He's not here." She stopped there, not feeling the need to explain her father's situation to a stranger. Her eyes darted to the gate set into the privacy fence surrounding the yard. He'd closed it. Fear crawled through her as she heard the echo of Sheriff Tompkins' earlier words: *Either he acted in a manner that had adverse consequences, or someone else did this to him.*

Nosy neighbors aside, the backyard remained secluded, and she did not know this man. What if Papa hadn't had a natural health crisis? What if this guy had already "found" him, much as he had now found her? Her thoughts went back to those seeming grip marks on her father's arm.

Before the stranger could react, she darted wide around him, expecting to be grabbed at any moment. She reached the stoop unhindered and retreated into the house, slamming and locking the back door behind her.

"Hey!" she heard the stranger call out. Almost immediately, he started to knock. Normal, not violent, but her pulse still quickened with each bang. He called to her again. She couldn't make out his words through the thick door, not that she hung around to try.

Hurrying to the front hall to grab her cell phone, Sheridan headed for the basement family room, afraid to go out the front in case he wasn't alone. She dialed the sheriff's office as she went, only, the sudden ring of an old-fashioned landline made her fumble her phone down the stairs before she could complete the call. Scowling at the offending contraption, she stepped into the stairwell and locked the basement door behind her. She stood at the top of the stairs and listened. The ringing stopped at five rings. After a brief pause, she heard her father's recorded voice kick in, making her heart twinge at the unexpected sound as the equally antique answering machine picked up.

"Um... hello? Please, pick up. I didn't mean to startle you, but I need to speak to Richard. I'm his assistant. The data that came through last night... it's like nothing we've recorded before. Hello? Please, tell Richard that Jac..."

And the machine cut out, the tape spool apparently full.

Sheridan stood there, feeling foolish, waiting for the next attempt from... *Jack*? At least, she assumed he was telling her his name. Should she trust him? Or was this a ruse?

She didn't quite know what to do. Until she'd heard his message, she'd had no clue who he was—or *might* be. How would she know? Papa had kept her isolated from his research. She still didn't know why. Would she ever?

A few minutes passed, then a few more, and nothing happened. The taut silence ticked on with only the faint sounds of a house at rest and the blare of Sheridan's thoughts. She wasn't good with spontaneous encounters at the best of times, let alone after being startled by a stranger, but she regretted fleeing. If this was Papa's research assistant, he seemed to have no idea anything was wrong. She huffed out a sigh. Presuming Jack was as he seemed, he might be able to help her figure out what was going on. And she'd blown the opportunity. Or had she?

Scampering down the stairs, she grabbed her phone and went back up again. With the number for the sheriff's office still cued up and her finger poised over the call button, she unlocked the basement door and eased it open. No one lunged at her. And nothing moved. Sheridan felt so foolish. She could blame it on little sleep and lots of stress, but excuses never accomplished anything. Time to stop being ridiculous.

A self-administered mental shove sent her toward the back door. She peered through the glass pane. No sign of Jack. Frowning, she disengaged the lock and stepped outside.

"Hello?" she called, grimacing as her voice came out a mere squeak. She cleared her throat and tried again. "Hello? Are you still there?"

Squaring her shoulders, she left the safety of the house before she could second-guess herself. Something crackled beneath her feet as she stepped onto the stoop. Sheridan moved to the side and knelt down. Her brow dipped. Half a brick held a sheath of computer printouts in place. They were the papers Jack had been holding. She scanned the sheets. At the top, Jack had scrawled: *Pls give to R*. Other than that, the streams of numbers, line graphs, and other sciency-looking notations were lost on her, but she presumed they would make sense to her father. She gathered them up and brushed off the dirt from the bottom of her shoe before turning and going back inside.

She should leave these on Papa's desk, but eighteen years of being forbidden access were difficult to shake. Of course, somewhere among his papers, she might find a way to contact Jack, or perhaps something else that would point her to an explanation. It was silly, really. Part of her still felt it would be unforgivable to trespass on Papa's private sanctum, the seat of his research, from which he'd adamantly kept her separate. Another part held tight to the belief that final bastion was her last slim hope of understanding what had happened before she was forced to accept there was little possibility of his recovery.

She really did *not* want to make that call.

Whatever secrets that room held, they were her last chance because there was nowhere left to search after that.

Chapter Nine

Days later, Jack hadn't returned or called again, but Sheridan continued to struggle with entering her father's study. Was it the fear that nothing she did would make a difference? Or the ingrained fact that she was not—and never *had* been—allowed inside that one room?

Worse yet, was it the looming possibility that her trespass wouldn't mean a thing because Papa would never recover enough to know of it?

Shaking off that grim thought, Sheridan headed for her childhood room. With her foot, she pushed aside her bags, which she'd dropped inside the door when she'd arrived and still hadn't moved. This wasn't the wisest thing she could do given her recent encounters with Katie... excuse me... *Kate*. But pretending the past didn't exist hadn't altered it. Better to confront the memories than to ignore them.

In silence, she scanned the room. Nothing had changed. In fact, if she had to guess, this was the first time anyone had been in there in the last five years. Posters of Nickelback and Jared Padalecki still festooned the walls, not wires. The only electronics were her old iPod dangling half off the dresser and an ancient *Gateway* laptop open and waiting for her on her desk beneath five years of dust. Staring at it all was like a slap in the face. As if from the moment she'd been gone, Papa had forgotten about her. He hadn't, but you couldn't tell from the condition of her room.

Sheridan shook off her doubts and took a deep, focusing breath.

She had no idea how long she would be here, but she knew it would drive her nuts to live out of her luggage. Hauling her suitcase off the floor and onto the bed, she unpacked her things. When she pulled open one of the dresser drawers, the forgotten remnants of her youth confronted her again as she discovered neatly folded jeans and tee shirts still nestled inside. With a frown, she set aside the clothes she'd brought with her and began to sort through the things she'd left behind, tossing them into three piles on the floor: *Not a chance, maybe good,* and *keeping it either way*. When she was done with the dresser, she moved to the closet. As she opened the creaking door, she gasped and rocked back, her hand reaching out to grip the plastic-protected dress hanging there, waiting for a night long past...

Sheridan could hardly believe it. Tomorrow, she – the Queen of the Outcasts – had a date to the Senior Prom. And she wasn't going by herself or with the other social pariahs who hadn't been asked... or asked each other, so they didn't look lame. She had an honest-to-goodness date!

She might never fall asleep tonight.

With a grin, she stripped down to her panties, bra, and her mother's pendant. She then carefully extracted her new electric-blue gown from its plastic-draped hanger. At first, she just held it up, hugging it to her slight curves, admiring the look and feel, but it wasn't enough. Sheridan couldn't resist. Taking great care, she slipped the zipper down and stepped into the dress, sliding her arms into the straps and contorting like crazy to zip the back as high as she could reach.

She frowned at her reflection. Not at the dress or how she looked in it, but at her necklace, framed by the fancy fabric looking so out of place in the open. Reaching up, she fingered the pendant... the yantra. She hadn't thought about it in practically forever. Her memories of that long-ago time were shrouded in shadow, always had been. From time to time, resurfacing in bits and pieces. But she knew Mama had given her the necklace and that she wasn't to take it off. But surely, in the privacy of her room...

For the first time since Mama placed it around her neck, Sheridan removed the pendant and hung it from the corner of her mirror. She shivered and told herself it was just for a moment. And then she took a good look at herself.

Her eyes shone, and a grin unfurled on her lips.

For the first time in her life, she felt normal. Special even.

Stepping back, she twirled in front of the mirror. So perfect! All sparkles and sleek, silky fabric, not too long, not too full. And just a few shades off from Jaxon's eyes. She'd been lucky to find a dress so perfect on short notice. She hadn't planned on going at all. Would Jaxon wear a cummerbund to match? Or settle for finding her a corsage and himself a boutonniere in a complementary shade? Was it too late for that? She hadn't felt brave enough to say anything. Shocked he had even asked her and not wanting to jinx it.

She liked him. She really, really liked him. And the way his deep chuckles made her toes tingle all the way up to… there… though she'd never admit that out loud.

He was new to their school, only just starting after winter break. Tall and cute, but quiet, with sandy brown hair and bright blue eyes. He mostly kept to himself, dropped in the middle of a senior class that had pretty much gone through every grade together since pre-k. No doubt Katie and the others had at least warned him about the weirdo freak, but he'd asked Sheridan to Prom anyway. And to be fair, she hadn't said or done anything freakish since the sixth grade. But still, she hoped, she really hoped with everything inside her, that this wasn't a cruel joke.

Reluctantly, she took the dress off and returned it to its hanger. Restoring the plastic, she tucked the dress inside her closet, on the hook on the back of the door.

Then, still lost in her daydreaming, she readied for bed, sliding between the sheets and pulling her extra pillow in for a hug, squealing at the thought of tomorrow. Rolling over, she snuggled into her blankets and hummed the latest Nickelback song, picturing Jaxon and her dancing beneath the cornball streamers and balloon arches that disguised the high school's gym.

Without noticing, daydreams slid into slumber, and true dreams transformed her imaginings into a whirl of sparkly lights and muted colors, the faint echo of music in her ears and shy, powerful glances from the boy she had started to crush on. They whirled and twirled and jostled in the crowd until the student body current slowly separated them.

Sheridan whimpered and reached out, but Jaxon disappeared among the bopping dancers, and someone else slipped into his place, a dark mass backlit by the party lights, every feature obscured. A hand reached out and intercepted Sheridan's. She tensed as the music took on a harder beat and the dancing morphed into a thrashing of bodies. Her head spun, and she tried to pull away, but the stranger's grip tightened on her wrist, digging in like claws as he yanked her closer, lifting her until somehow her feet left the dance floor, and she lost all purchase to resist. Each tug drew her higher until it seemed she looked down on a frozen tableau.

A gasp escaped her throat. Below she spied a shadow figure looming above a girl in electric blue. Her head snapped up to her assailant, nothing but a silhouette and a flash of red glowing eyes. Malevolent satisfaction enveloped her, robbing her of breath, trapping her in the stranger's gaze. The students milling below faded into an afterimage as each moment passed. Sheridan's chest tightened, and her muscles locked as the world she knew began to vanish, and *darkness crept in. In silence, she screamed. Willing her hand to tug free, her soul cried out for help.*

Like the flash of an old-fashioned camera, an orb lit the space between Sheridan and the Shadow Man. Its sudden brilliance banished the darkness, forcing it away. The tight grip on her wrist abruptly released. Sheridan had the sensation of tumbling, though she didn't seem to move at all. Instinctively, she squeezed her eyes closed as she willed herself back into her body, only to stop as she caught an impression of a delicate, feminine face turned back toward her, her glance wistful and melancholy, features for a moment limned in glowing light...

Those features... so achingly familiar Sheridan feared to lay a name to them. As she reached out to the brilliance, a muffled crash, like a door slamming open, dropped her down, back into her body like a stone into a pond. The sudden return to reality weighed heavy on her. Still robbed of breath, she arched, gasping until her airways opened, then thudded back down on her mattress. Disoriented, she slowly shook her head. A sharp click *sounded, and the ceiling light flashed on. She squinted against the brightness, her head turning toward the door. Her father stood there, eyes wide and panicked. He looked more terrified than she felt.*

"Gone... You were almost gone!" Papa's breath hitched, and he gripped the door frame as if to steady himself. "Not again. I can't bear that again..."

The next morning, well before her alarm would have sounded to wake her up for school, she and her father were on the road to Aunt Bonnie's house in Denver.

Sheridan never did wear the electric-blue dress or get to go to Prom.

With a sob, she shook off the memory and returned to herself, her body trembling and her left hand fisted in the plastic-draped dress that triggered the flashback. Through the faded ink of her tattoo, three black marks like fingerprints barely stood out. But even if they hadn't, she would have known they were there as she had every day since they appeared on her skin that impossible night.

Chapter Ten

Sheridan couldn't say how long she stood in the hallway. How long she listened to the faint ticking of the pendulum clock on the far side of the door. Long enough to be standing in a pool of fading sunlight when she'd started out in shadow. Evening approached. And still, she just stood there, staring at the gleaming brass knob, worn as soft as satin by generations of her family's hands.

As she worked up the courage to enter the forbidden sanctum, she thought she saw another flash from the corner of her eye, but when she turned, there was only the wire-draped hallway leading deeper into the house, steeped in shadow broken only by red pinpoints of light flashing back to green. Even so, the afterimage of a glowing orb still teased her vision. Just off to the side. Seen, but not seen.

A ripple of nerves danced beneath her skin. Sheridan straightened her shoulders and tightened her jaw. Her time of jumping at shadows — or glowing orbs — was done. She reached out and opened the door, tensing a moment as it creaked, before shaking her head at her folly.

Who was there to hear? Who was there to care? Certainly, not her father. He lay still and unresponsive in his hospital bed, and if something in this room could tell her how to help him when all mundane efforts had failed, she was damned well going to search it from baseboard to crown molding and everything in between. She might not have the education or training to understand most of what she found, but all she needed was a direction to look, and she would find the answers.

Entering her father's study, being inside the room for the first time... Well... the only way to describe it was a let-down. She'd expected more. Grandeur or sciency stuff. Academic citations on the walls. Polished wood and a high-tech computer. What she found was an industrial desk like those her high school teachers had manned, with a chaotic mound of… *stuff* covering the surface. Charts and diagrams papered the walls where overflowing bookcases didn't already cover them. Her father's scribble annotated the margins of most of them. And then there were the books. So many books. And journals and notebooks and scraps of paper liberally scribbled over, interspersed with junk mail and what looked disturbingly like bills. An old-fashioned banker's lamp perched on Papa's desk, looking way too grand for its surroundings. Everything else was make-do except for the globe in the corner, which she noticed cracked open to reveal a minibar.

With hesitation, she entered. For a moment, she closed her eyes and breathed deep, taking in the scents of paper and ink and Papa's favorite—if difficult to find—Black Jack gum. Sheridan couldn't stand the stuff herself, but the sharp signature smell of anise wrapped her like a hug in her father's arms.

When she opened her eyes, the rest of the room hit her like sensory overload, the mingled scents, the sharp tick of the clock, the slight, damp funk on the air that made her wonder if half-filled dishes and mugs hid in here as well…

It was too much.

Baby steps. She needed to exercise this rebellion in baby steps, not all at once.

Moving deeper into the room, she ran a hand over a shelf of small leather personal journals. Papa's "diaries," as she'd always thought of them, though who knew what kind of "secrets" they held. She never dreamed of looking inside them as a child, not that he left them lying about. Even now, she couldn't bring herself to violate Papa's privacy to that great an extent. As it was, she fought the impulse to skedaddle out of the study before she got caught.

Instead, she took out her cell phone and moved to the one wall not lined by bookshelves. In the center hung a map of the US with added lines and circles bisecting most of the delineated borders. She snapped pictures of the map and the pages of notes and diagrams surrounding it on the wall, smiling as, among them, she came across random drawings she'd given her father over the years, noticing he'd written on them as well, but not paying them much mind. Once she had photographed everything, she searched for the hidden biohazards in the room, stacking those she located in an empty trash bin to carry out.

Wrinkling her nose and wishing she'd brought kitchen gloves in with her, Sheridan ventured behind the desk, searching for a noxious aroma. What she found was a thick stack of her early drawings. Her breath came a little faster as she realized they resembled her reactive sketches. All of them, she would guess, though she hadn't come to think of them that way until she was much older. Art from her youngest days up, created after one shadow episode or another.

She lowered herself into Papa's chair, brushing a finger across a note her father had scrawled in the margin of the top image. *Hooded Monk (yellow?),* he'd written beside a man-shape scribble that appeared to be wearing a cowl. Using the barest touch, she shifted the top image away, shuddering at the one beneath it; a woman's silhouette, hair scraggly and long, perched on top of a person in a six-year-old's depiction of a bed. *Old Hag (purple?),* her father wrote.

The pile—and the notes—went on.

On one of the images toward the bottom—she must have been older when she'd drawn it. Ten? Twelve?—Papa had written, *So many different depictions. Has she truly seen them all? And so clearly? How?*

Why are they drawn to my daughter?

What did Papa mean, "drawn to her"? Depictions of what? Feeling unsteady, Sheridan picked up the bin and the stack of drawings and left the room.

Baby steps. Friggin' *baby steps!*

Chapter Eleven

Next to the hospital, Sheridan had discovered the new-to-her Cooper Memorial Park, open to the public and close enough to give families and ambulatory patients a break from their stressful surroundings. She'd taken advantage of that ever since, fleeing her father's room when the silence weighed too heavily upon her. It had been a week since she'd arrived, and she felt adrift, with nowhere to turn to sort things out. That day, she started the day in the park, stretching her legs on paths lined by cultivated spring flowers and bushes allowed to go wild, trying to gain some Zen *before* sitting vigil beside her father.

The weather was nice today. Families and couples dotted the open field on blankets or bare grass while serious and not-so-serious games played out on the ball fields in the distance. Sheridan stood behind the protective fence a while, watching what appeared to be Little League practice, when she noticed a pick-up game breaking up the next field over. One of the players caught her eye. Or rather, his eyes did, bright blue and startlingly familiar.

She drew her lower lip between her teeth. It could be him... Papa's research assistant. Or it could be a complete stranger. By the time she made up her mind, he had started walking away.

In a panic, she hurried forward, crying out, "Jack!"

For a brief instant, everyone stopped before most of them continued on. The blue-eyed man, however, pivoted and turned her way, his brow furrowed. When his gaze locked on hers, she would swear a mix of relief and startlement flitted across his expression, ending in a brilliant smile.

"Oh, my god," Sheridan swayed, nearly falling as he jogged toward her, and recognition kicked in. How had she missed it before? "It's you..."

Looking sheepish as he stopped before her, Jaxon nodded. "It's me."

"Why didn't you say something at the house?"

Sheridan watched Jaxon's ears take on a slight neon-pink hue. "I didn't realize you were *you* until after I... left."

Fair enough, it had been five years.

"And why didn't you come back?"

"I heard about Richard, and I didn't know what to do."

Sheridan barked a half-hearted laugh. "That makes two of us. Um... I am so sorry about how I reacted the other day. My imagination got the better of me..."

Jaxon smiled and waved off her apology. "No worries, you can't be too careful these days."

"Thank you," she said, smiling back. "So, do you have to rush off, or do you have some time to catch up with the weirdo freak who keeps taking off on you?"

As soon as the words were out of her mouth, she wanted to cringe. Her attempt to lighten things up did anything but.

"Unique, not freak," Jaxon protested, a faint frown rippling his brow. Then he nodded. An easy smile replaced the frown. "I don't need to be anywhere right now."

Sheridan flushed at his protest but relaxed as he turned and gestured in the direction of the path leading toward the lake at the center of the park. "Shall we?"

A faint smile found its way to Sheridan's lips despite her embarrassment. She nodded and fell into step beside him, awed at the ease with which they interacted. Almost as if five years ago hadn't happened. Jaxon slid his hands into his pockets and dropped into a relaxed pace. They went a ways around Bradbury Lake in silence before Sheridan couldn't help herself. "How in holy hell did you end up working with my father?"

That startled a laugh out of Jaxon.

"We met through a sleep study at the university. I was a research assistant to one of the doctors there. Richard volunteered as one of the test subjects."

That made sense, given their history with sleep issues. It also explained all of the academic journals she'd found in Papa's study, with article after article about sleep disorders flagged.

"When did you realize he was my father?"

"Ah... I didn't, until quite recently," Jaxon answered, looking down at the path as his shoulders tensed. "He and I had never actually met before."

He graciously left it at that, but Sheridan felt mortified, realizing that Jaxon hadn't gotten to meet her father because they were halfway to Denver around the time he would have arrived to pick up her up for the Prom.

She stopped walking and waited for him to turn back to her. He looked concerned as he closed the distance between them. "What's wrong?"

Sheridan swallowed hard, her throat suddenly dry. "I am also sorry about Prom," she managed, but he waved any explanation she might have given away.

"We were kids. Neither of us had any control beyond what our parents allowed us. Don't worry. I just ditched the dance and headed to the beach for Skip Day a few days early."

She envied him those experiences nearly as much as she envied his relaxed attitude about the matter. He could have held a grudge. Bad enough being stood up for the Senior Prom, but being stood up by the weirdo freak? Quite a blow to a teen reputation, or so she imagined. At least he hadn't had to deal with it long.

When Sheridan remained silent, not knowing what to say, Jaxon cocked his head and lifted his brow. "Are we okay?" he asked, spreading his arms as if to say, "what's up?"

Giving a little laugh, she nodded.

"Good. Now tell me what you've been doing with your life."

It was Sheridan's turn to tense. She could think of nothing worth the telling. She never had returned to school, GEDing out as soon as she reached Denver rather than trying to acclimate to a new, much larger school weeks before graduation. She'd gotten a job and stayed with Aunt Bonnie—who hadn't been thrilled when they'd shown up on her doorstep—only long enough to save a deposit and first and last month's rent for an apartment before striking out on her own. Neither of them had told Papa. Eventually, Sheridan put herself through art school, but for the most part, life had been never-ending efforts to stay fed and clothed and sheltered. Not exactly carefree conversation.

"Not much," she answered, keeping it light. "Getting by, making art, teaching some, and right now, trying to make sense of my father's research, to figure out why he was up in the foothills and what might have happened when he got there."

Jaxon gave her a gentle smile, something in his gaze telling her he understood. "Sounds good. Now, how about I help you see what sense we can make of the notes Richard left behind?"

Sheridan winced. She hadn't been to the hospital to see her father yet, but she wasn't about to inflict that whole situation on Jaxon. It wasn't like her father was even aware she was there. Raising a silent apology to Papa, she said, "Sure, let's go."

Side by side, they cut across the green space, heading for the parking lot.

Chapter Twelve

By tacit agreement, Jaxon followed her home in his car. She pulled in and opened the garage, tucking the Prius inside to charge, making room for Jaxon's Dodge Ramcharger in the driveway. With a shiver, her gaze went to the stairs leading to her loft. Her thoughts returned to her early drawings. The ones she'd found in the study. What had Papa seen in them? And what did any of that have to do with his research?

Part of her was afraid to know.

Brushing away those thoughts, she stepped outside and locked the garage.

When she turned, Jaxon waited by the stoop, his hands in his pockets and a backpack over his shoulder. That seemed to be his default around spooked women. Or maybe just her. After all, she had freaked out the last time they stood here.

There were worse things. But not much.

Aiming a wry grin in his direction, she stepped past him to climb the steps to the back door, purposely bumping his shoulder with hers as she passed.

He chuckled, and her toes sent a sharp tingle upward. She gasped at the long-forgotten reaction, then blushed, hoping Jaxon didn't see it, though he had no way of knowing the cause.

Keeping her face turned away, she unlocked the back door and led the way in, very glad she'd cleaned the place up over the last few days. Even so, Jaxon gave a long, low whistle at the sight of the dining room table and the web of electronics veining the walls.

"Ah, yeah," Sheridan said to his unspoken comment. "It used to be a *lot* worse. There's more in the other room I haven't sorted yet. How about you get started here while I go tackle the mountain?"

Jaxon nodded as he heaved a deep breath and set his bag on the floor by the kitchen table. "Yeah, how about I make some coffee first? Pretty sure I see a pot hiding behind that stack over there."

Sheridan winced, not even wanting to go into the fate of the former kitchenware. "Um... coffee pot, check... Coffee mugs... not anymore. Just paper goods."

"Don't worry, we'll make it work. How about coffee?"

"Freezer," she said with a relieved grin, glad she had stocked up. "Want me to throw together some sandwiches? I don't know about you, but breakfast was a long time ago."

"Sounds like a plan."

Sheridan turned the under-the-counter radio on low as she slipped past him to the fridge, taking out the mayo, Dijon, and lettuce and tomato, setting them on the counter to go back in for the turkey and sharp cheddar slices. "White or rye?"

"Either's good."

"Hand me the rye," she asked. "It's right there in the bread box next to the sugar bowl."

As he passed it overhand, like a basketball, Sheridan laughed. *This feels nice. Real nice.* It had been a long time since she'd had anyone to goof off with, let alone share meal prep, not that it had been all that common before.

They ate off paper plates at the now-cleared kitchen table, with an open bag of chips between them. Though, to be honest, Sheridan had a bit of trouble with the coffee, not realizing how hard the reminder would hit her after her conversation with Dr. Varughese. She pushed the doubled paper cup away and got up to get some water.

Jaxon frowned, his expression one of concern. "Everything okay?"

"Ah... yeah," Sheridan answered, not wanting to go into it. "Just, coffee and I aren't such good friends right now."

"O-kay..." With one more considering look in her direction, he popped the last bite of his sandwich in his mouth, chewing and swallowing to rival any teenage boy, before shouldering his pack and rising to his feet. "We're losing daylight. We better get started."

Sheridan smiled her thanks at the redirect and finished getting her water from the filter attachment on the spigot before gathering some supplies from beneath the sink.

Together they returned to the dining room.

"Sooo..." she started, the word drawing out as she tried to work out where to start. "Three piles." She pointed to each. "Scientific research... strange occurrences... everything else."

Jaxon nodded. Sliding out a chair from the table, he sat, pulling a notepad and pen from his pack before setting it on the floor. Then, without hesitation, he pulled the science pile toward him. "I'll go through the easy stuff first."

She quirked a brow at that. "If you say so."

He barely noticed. Shaking her head, she left him head-down in the piles, his right hand scribbling away on a notepad. Comforted by Jaxon's presence, she once again breached Papa's inner sanctum, this time armed with a couple of canvas shopping bags and a pair of kitchen gloves tucked into her waistband.

The status quo ingrained in her even after all of these years, Sheridan closed the study door behind her. Looking at the desk and her father's chair behind it, she could not bring herself to violate that space again so soon. Instead, she shifted the accumulation from what nominally would have been the guest chair in front of it—if her father had ever let anyone in—and perched on the edge, setting one canvas bag to either side of her, open to receive whatever she found that was worthy. She reached over and tugged the chain on the banker's lamp, filling the space where she sat with a warm downward glow, tempered by the thick, green shade.

She took a moment to adjust to the world not ending because she sat there, then dug in.

After a few hours, her nose twitched continually from the disturbed dust. With a sigh, Sheridan blew the hair out of her eyes and kept sorting, part of her certain she would find no bottom to the pile, only endless layers of the indecipherable. Anything with notes, highlights, or sticky notes she set into the bag on her right. Mail—junk and otherwise—went into the bag at her left. Anything not marked up in some way started a fresh, organized pile beside the desk. As the sunlight transitioned across the room, she lost track of time, entranced by her task and the steady tick of the pendulum clock on the wall. She did manage to uncover a sliver of desk. A patch about the size of a dinner plate.

Her stomach gave a loud rumble at the tenuous reminder that the next mealtime was in danger of passing by disregarded. Sheridan ignored it for now. She wanted to clear away a little more before calling it a night. Diving into another pile, she lost herself in the cycle of flip and scan and sort, looking for Papa's annotations and sticky notes to give her insight into his thought process when he undertook whatever mad experiment he'd fallen victim to.

The natural light had fled the room when Sheridan uncovered another shock, an old, framed picture. Thirty years, at least. The kind of thing they'd taken at school dances in the '80s. It took her a moment to recognize her father's face beneath the classic mullet. She laughed and traced his features lovingly with a finger. But as her gaze drifted to the other person in the picture—who she knew would have been her mother, Mary—all mirth faded.

Leaning closer to the light, Sheridan held the picture at different angles, shifting to avoid the glare on the glass, not understanding what she saw. The smiling girl staring out of the picture bore a faint similarity to her mother as Sheridan remembered her. Like a cousin or a sister. More like Aunt Bonnie. Everything was right to Sheridan's artistic eye: the shape, the features, the proportions, but even taking into account changing styles and age progression, something about the woman's gaze screamed "stranger!"

Sheridan would swear to it, though she couldn't identify who or how... or why.

She continued to scour the photograph for clarity, but as she did, Sheridan felt a presence behind her. How had she not heard the door open? Or even Jaxon's footsteps coming down the hall? However he had managed to sneak up on her, she found it surprising that it had taken him this long to step in and drag her away from her task. Perhaps he'd been as lost in dissecting the contents of the dining room table?

"Just a minute," she muttered. "I'm almost finished."

She barely noticed that he didn't respond, but her shoulders tensed at the patient presence at her back.

"Please, I'll be right out."

A tingle ran down her spine as a hand brushed her shoulder, the sensation slight and a bit cool. She shuddered, darting a glance, but she could see nothing in the gloom beyond her little bubble of light. She turned back to her piles as the hand withdrew, along with the sense of his presence. Sheridan still did not hear the door open or close. For some reason, the thought that he may have left it open bothered her. A throwback to her childhood, perhaps, when Papa had kept it closed, whether he was inside or not.

She shrugged a little in annoyance. Tucking the picture into the bag on her right, she turned, blinking at the sight of the closed door. A frown tugged the corners of her mouth as she reached down, picked up the shopping bag with her father's notes and the photograph, and stood, resigned that the night's efforts were done. Leaving the circle of light cast by the desk lamp, she crossed the darkened room to the door and, by the light of the red and green sensors lining the hallway, moved through the house toward the dining room.

"Jaxon?"

No answer.

"Hey, Jaxon, where'd you go?"

The light from the dining room glowed like a beacon ahead of her. Sheridan moved through the archway and stopped short. Beneath the light's warmth, Jaxon lay with his head resting on a pile of academic journals like Sleeping Beauty pricked at her spinning wheel. His back rose and fell with the low, steady breaths of deep slumber. Sheridan's chest tightened at the sight, and her free hand slapped out at the wall, searching for the light switch, no longer comfortable with the dark at her back.

Chapter Thirteen

Entering the dining room, Sheridan dragged a chair out of her way, making noise without startling a month's worth of days off Jaxon's life.

"Wakey, wakey, Prince Charming!" she called out with forced cheer and exuberance, her mind still locked on the Sleeping Beauty reference, only to flinch as she realized what she'd called him. Fortunately, her words didn't seem to have registered. He raised his head and blinked away the sleep, grimacing comically as he peeled a sticky note from his cheek.

"Come on, Jaxon, let's go get some food."

He smiled up at her, looking way too adorable, all sleepy and rumpled. "Sounds like a plan!" Getting to his feet, he stretched, his fingers almost brushing the ceiling. Blushing and averting her eyes as his muscles flexed, Sheridan moved past him toward the kitchen when a frame on the sideboard caught her eye. She frowned. It used to hang on the wall, but now the frame looked damaged, imperfectly repaired. It held a family portrait from when she was one. She moved closer, pulling the older photo from the tote bag and holding it up in comparison.

She hadn't imagined it.

Something essential had changed in Mary Cascaden between the school photograph and the portrait.

With a slight frown, Sheridan ran a finger over the picture of the three of them. A familiar chain hung around Mama's neck, the end tucked beneath her shirt. The pendant Mama had given her. Where had it gone? Even after all these years, Sheridan felt its absence like an ache in her chest. Somehow, she had lost it between the rush to leave home and arriving in Denver. Maybe it was here, forgotten with the other remnants of her teenage life. Maybe it was gone forever. Either way, she seemed to have gotten along just fine without it. And yet, her heart ached. And her gut clenched.

She had given Mama her promise but had not kept it.

Sheridan tried to shake the sense of foreboding. She slipped the picture from the study back into her bag and continued on her way out, flicking on light switches as she passed even though they were leaving. She started to grab Papa's keys from the key-tray in the kitchen when Jaxon spoke up.

"How about I drive," he offered. "Unless you're aiming for breakfast instead of dinner…?"

His tone was all innocence, but Sheridan gave him the stink eye over her shoulder, well aware he poked fun at her seeming inability to navigate the streets of current-day Bradbury without getting turned around, which she'd mentioned in frustration when they'd been chatting earlier, catching up on what had changed (way too much) and what had stayed the same (just enough to be vexing) since she'd been gone.

"Whatever."

He laughed, and some of the tension knotting her shoulders loosened.

Leaving the keys where they were, Sheridan stepped to the side and let Jaxon precede her out the door. She was about to follow him when something flickered to her left at the corner of her eye, movement in the pool of darkness that was the sunroom at night. Quickly, not moving save for her arm, Sheridan flicked the switch on the wall beside her.

Expecting brightness, she received disappointment.

A bare bulb beside the door sent out a weak glow as the ceiling fan ramped up to speed. The light provided as much shadow as it did illumination, making it impossible to identify what might have moved in the darkness.

Sheridan jumped with a gasp as more movement flickered to her right from the kitchen.

"Hey, what's up? You okay?"

Settling herself with a deep breath, Sheridan waited a beat before answering.

"I'm fine. Let's go."

As she followed Jaxon back out the door, the situation nagged at her. Locking the door as she exited, she stopped on the stoop and turned to Jaxon.

"Did my father get a cat?"

Jaxon looked first confused and then uncomfortable. "Um… we aren't friends, Sheridan… Richard and I," he quickly clarified. "I help him out with computations to supplement my internship. Occasionally, I do some data-crunching and research, but mostly we do our own thing and communicate by email. I don't even know what he does with the stuff I compile for him. Heck, I only know where he lives because as much as this place has changed, Bradbury is still a small town, and everyone talks."

What little comfort she'd garnered from knowing Papa had *someone* in his life flaked away.

"Why?" she asked.

He shrugged and looked contrite, though he had no reason to be. "It's all he ever wanted.

"Don't get me wrong, I like him. It's just… I don't think anyone knows him."

Sheridan swallowed hard. *Not even me.* She shook off a wave of melancholy and resisted the urge to ask if *they* were friends or not. "Okay… So, food?"

Jaxon watched her a moment, long and considering, before nodding. "Food." And he led her to his truck, opening the door and setting her tote in the footwell before helping her up. He then closed the door and hurried around to the driver's side to climb behind the wheel. Though he slid the key into the ignition, he didn't start it up.

Turning toward him, Sheridan asked, "Everything okay?"

He nodded but pressed his lips together, fumbling with something in his pocket.

"I found this in the kitchen when I went back for more coffee," he said as he held out a well-worn book. "I thought it might help us, but it looks more personal than professional."

Sheridan froze. She knew that book. And many others like it. Papa's little leather journals that he had scribbled in every day for as far back as she could remember. Sheridan had noticed a whole shelf of them in the study. He'd started carrying them everywhere after Mama disappeared, writing in them more than ever, his expression at times fierce, at others worried, but always distant.

Almost as if on its own, her hand reached out, her fingers just skimming across the dusty leather. Jaxon moved the journal closer to her, encouraging her to take it.

If she'd had a difficult time entering Papa's study, just accepting this book felt like a worse infraction without her having even opened its cover.

Sheridan's hand shook as it closed around the thick volume.

As much as she longed to open it, all she could do was stroke the cover.

Jaxon still had not started the truck. He sat there waiting patiently.

The atmosphere in the cab thickened until Sheridan felt herself twitch as if to dispel the increasing tension. The awkwardness built, layer by layer, fed by her silence.

And still, Jaxon didn't rush her.

Sighing, Sheridan gathered her courage and flipped open the journal. She swayed in her seat as her gaze landed on the first line:

We buried Mary today.

The single line repeated over and over in her head until it blended into an angry buzz.

If not for the sound, she might have heard Jaxon cry out before the darkness rose like a wave and smashed her down.

Chapter Fourteen

Seven was kind of old to have to hold Papa's hand, but Sheridan didn't question. She stood there and listened to the low rumble of voices without hearing any words. She wanted to know why she had to stand there at all when all she wanted... when all she wanted...

Her muzzy brain wouldn't finish the thought.

She stood there and let it all drift past her like a blurred and boring dream she was too tired to remember. When Papa moved, she shuffled forward. Otherwise, her thoughts scattered like dandelion fluff on the wind. In fact, she barely noticed as he reached down and hauled her up in his arms, moving past masses of murmuring people to a clear space at the front of the room.

Sheridan leaned into him, taking comfort from his warm and solid mass, but as she did, her cheek pressed against his, and her little brow furrowed to find it cool and wet. When had the rain come? But it hadn't. They were inside. Her free hand skimmed down the skirt of her dress and encountered only stiff dry cotton. "Papa?" was all she managed, the word rounder and softer than usual as her tongue and lips resisted the effort to speak.

"Shhh..." he murmured back, his voice... cracking, she thought, though it was difficult to tell as her mind wandered. But he held her tight and brushed a kiss across her brow as he moved them forward, so she settled into the comfort of his arms and did not let herself be bothered by anything around her.

Until he stopped.

Sheridan blinked woozily as she looked down in front of them. At first, a bit of spark resurfaced, a distant but determined joy, as she saw her mother resting there. She wiggled a bit, arching and leaning forward, wanting to get down to snuggle, but Papa's grip tightened, and if she weren't so focused on her goal, she might have realized the sudden cries she heard sobbed out in his voice.

Papa spun away, clutching her against his chest as she reached out to where Mama lay so peacefully. Gripped by overwhelming anguish, Sheridan cried out...

"Shhh... Shhh..." a deep voice rumbled beneath her ear as a loose grip tightened around her. Sheridan barely heard, choking on her own sobs as her heart fractured as it never had before. She felt the sensation of being lifted from prone to semi-upright as whoever she lay against scooched up and drew her with him. "It's okay, Sher. I promise it's going to be okay."

That *wasn't* Papa.

Struggling to breathe, she pushed away from whoever held her, putting distance between them, her balance precarious on the edge of... a bed. *Where the hell was she?*

The person in the bed with her leaned away, the mattress shifting beneath him as he slid to the opposite edge and lowered a leg to the floor. He reached for the nightstand. Suddenly, a soft glow lit a bubble of space around them, emanating from what she realized was her phone. Jaxon stared back at her, fully clothed, if rumpled and perhaps a bit damp, though that didn't seem to concern him. From the look of it, they were in her bedroom, though she hadn't the foggiest how they ended up there.

Sheridan trembled and fought the urge to cry again, gnawing on her lower lip as she struggled for control.

"We were going to get food," she muttered.

"We were, but then you... passed out," Jaxon explained, keeping his tone soft, slow, and simple, giving her time to catch up. "I brought you inside and tried to wake you, but you were still, well... kind of out of it. Then I tried at least to lay you down, but you wouldn't let me."

Sheridan winced and dipped her head until her hair hid her face. Jaxon continued, remaining calm.

"You were upset. You wouldn't settle unless I," — and here he blushed — "unless I held you."

"She didn't die," Sheridan practically growled the words, looking up to pin Jaxon with a heated gaze. He looked confused.

"Who?"

"Mama," she bit off the word. "I don't care what Papa wrote; I was there. She disappeared. The Shadow Man took her away. They buried the other Mary."

And if that didn't sound bat-shit crazy the more the fog lifted. But Sheridan refused to doubt what she *knew*, no matter if it sounded loony to anyone else. And then it hit her. Her subconscious had made sense of the puzzle before her mind had caught on. Sheridan now knew why the picture she'd found earlier felt wrong, like it was of someone else. Same body, but without the essence of what Sheridan knew as Mama. Like Papa in his hospital bed.

His expression nothing but concerned, Jaxon took her hand and rubbed soothing circles along the back of it. "What do you mean?"

Sheridan swallowed hard before answering. "The book. Papa's journal. The first thing it said was 'We buried Mary today.'" She swallowed again. "Mary is my mother's name. I remember now, but the book is wrong. That was Mama's body in that casket, but she was already gone."

"That's what happens when you die…"

"No!" Sheridan snatched her hand back, not caring as angry tears streamed down her face. "She didn't *die*. She's gone. I watched her go…"

Jaxon didn't argue the distinction again. Even so, Sheridan gritted her teeth and growled, fighting the urge to smack him. Knowing once again she sounded certifiable. That once again, she was the weirdo freak. But even in the low light of her phone, already dimming to conserve the battery, she saw no sign of judgment in Jaxon's gaze. No sign of wariness in his expression.

"She didn't die. The Shadow Man grabbed her and took her away," Sheridan repeated with full conviction. "And now the same thing has happened to Papa."

And still, Jaxon's expression did not flicker or waver, though the look he gave her sharpened, and he leaned closer.

"The shadow man? Do you mean you couldn't see who it was?"

Sheridan avoided his gaze. "No. I mean *the* Shadow Man. Like… a man cut out of the shadow. Blacker than black until I felt like I could reach out and touch him, only I couldn't move. Staring and poking until I wanted to scream, but the sound was trapped inside. I could see him from the corner of my eye, but he disappeared right through the wall when I tried to look at him straight on. And he took Mama with him!"

Jaxon leaned even closer, excitement gleaming in his eye even as the light from the phone went dimmer, making him a silhouette all too reminiscent of the subject of their discussion. "You see Shadow People?"

"Turn on the damn light!"

He leaned back, reaching behind him without looking away. His hand fumbled until it found the knob. Sheridan squinted against the sudden warm glow even as she relaxed at the return of the light.

"You think the shadows took your mother away?"

Sheridan snarled. She didn't *think* anything. She *knew*.

Before she could snap at him, he went taut, his eyes widening. He reached out as if he would grip her arm but thought better of it.

"You..." he nearly whispered, his voice practically vibrating. "It was *you*."

Sheridan moved a little further back, almost sliding off the bed. "Me?"

"The readings from the other day. Richard was already in the hospital. Those spectacular readings had to be you."

"I guess," she answered, twitching away from his intensity. "You said Shadow People like it's a thing. Is it a thing?"

Jaxon blinked and straightened, his head tilting slightly to the side. "Well. Yeah. It's one of the oldest unexplained phenomena. It goes back as far as recorded history. Besides, anyone in the field of sleep research has heard of Shadow People. Richard never talked to you about them?"

It took an effort not to scoff at his question. She and Papa hadn't ever talked about much beyond school or her art or if she'd done her chores. Certainly not anything to do with his research, or as she liked to think of it, his obsession. To be honest, she had lost more than her mother that long-ago night, or close enough.

"Not really," she said, rather than dump all of that on Jaxon.

"And you haven't looked them up?"

She frowned and looked away. "I was just a kid. How was I supposed to know it was a thing? I barely even remembered what happened until I saw that damned book. Besides, it's not like I need the internet to confirm I'm a weirdo freak."

"Hey, I thought we discussed this... unique, not freak."

"Oh, but you agree with the weirdo part?"

Grabbing her spare pillow, Jaxon swatted her with it. "That is a matter of opinion with which I do *not* agree, but it *is* open to debate."

Sheridan snatched the pillow away and swatted him back, grinning as the banter defused the building tension between them.

Jaxon's gaze softened.

"I'm sorry about your mother. It couldn't have been easy growing up without her."

Sheridan's grin faded, and she shifted where she sat. Over the years, she had heard countless variations of those words. This was the first time they sounded sincere. She didn't know how to respond. Jaxon just nodded and went on.

"How about I go get you some tea, and then we sit down and look through that book, see if we can't find some answers?"

Like a smack on the surface of a non-Newtonian fluid, Sheridan instantly tensed. She shook her head as she pushed off the bed, this time giving in to the impulse she had a week ago. "How about *you* sit down, and I go get the whiskey."

Jaxon barked a startled laugh, looking just a touch wary.

"Not on an empty stomach, after all of that..." He waved his hand in the air as if that covered everything. "So... Let's compromise. You go find that whiskey, and I'll go ready the tea and whatever I can scrounge from your fridge, and you meet me at the kitchen table."

Grudgingly, Sheridan nodded, leaning past him to snag her phone and Papa's journal before heading for the globe in the study, flicking on every light along the way.

Chapter Fifteen

Neither one of them ended up drinking much whiskey, not beyond a splash or two in their tea to steady them after all the turmoil. While Jaxon manned the tea kettle, Sheridan dove back into the fridge, hauling out some leftover barbeque, which she didn't bother heating up, homemade coleslaw, and a jar of crisp pickles. She set it all out on the table with more paper plates and a stack of napkins, then turned to Jaxon.

"What did you do with the tote I was carrying?"

He rolled his lips and looked up into nothing a moment before responding, "Still in the truck."

She held her hand out for his keys.

Jaxon nodded toward the key-tray, and Sheridan smiled, somehow moved by the gesture. Her heart fluttered just a little bit as she grabbed his keys and went out to retrieve the bag.

When she returned to the kitchen, they ate in silence, both of them looking wrung out by the earlier excitement. And when they were done, Jaxon pressed Sheridan back down in her seat as he got up to clear things away, nudging the journal closer to her once he collected her plate.

Sheridan didn't move to pick it up. What would be worse? To read those words and tear down the world as she knew it or pass it to Jaxon and have *him* privy to her screwed-up family secrets first.

Of course, the answer didn't matter. She had no choice but to read those pages. Jaxon wouldn't know what was significant or not. Propping her head up with one hand on her forehead, she pulled the journal closer, only to push it back and reach for the tote.

"I'm not ready for that," she said, not meeting Jaxon's gaze as she dumped the material she'd sifted from the study onto the table. "Let's go through this and see if anything jumps out at you."

"Okay." Jaxon pulled a pristine notepad out from a backpack on the seat beside him. As the flap lay open, Sheridan noticed a laptop.

"Hey, can I see that?"

He looked a little hesitant.

"Don't worry, I won't check your browser history," Sheridan teased. "I want to access my Gmail, so we can both look at the photos I took on my phone."

"Okay, just give me a second," he murmured as he powered the computer up. "What's your Gmail?"

"What? Seriously? I was joking!"

Jaxon winced a little. "It's a work computer. There are things on here I can't let you see."

Making a face, Sheridan jotted down her access information and waited as he logged in as her and went to Google Photos.

"Okay, come show me which to download."

She resisted being snotty as she came around and pointed at the ones he should click.

He whistled as the photo of the map filled his screen. "Wow… these are ley lines… and earthrings… and vortexes…" he said, his finger tracing each one as he identified them for her. "Some people believe they are places of mystical power and strange occurrences."

She couldn't resist. "Like Shadow People?"

Jaxon just nodded; his inner researcher caught up in the wealth of detail.

Sheridan studied the map over his shoulder. As best she could tell, ley lines and earthrings crisscrossed Bradbury like crazy, whereas Denver—where she'd been sent—fell in a dead zone between the lines but almost the bullseye of one of the rings. While she had no idea what that meant, she did know that Denver had, for the most part, proven to be an episode-free zone. And anything she had encountered there had been harmless, benevolent, even, much like she'd experienced as a child, whereas the malevolent had rarely disturbed her… until Mama went away. Suddenly, it made much more sense that Papa had sent her to Denver to keep her safe.

Between bites of ribs and slaw, she and Jaxon sorted through the rest, but nothing jumped out on its own as significant. They noted details that seemed to be pieces to the whole and then moved on.

Splitting the pile of papers and journals between them, they skimmed them in silence, occasionally sharing something of note. Jaxon's notepad could no longer be called pristine, and the one he'd pulled out for Sheridan had been similarly marked and folded.

"Get a load of this one," Sheridan said, breaking the silence, sharing one of the articles Papa had marked in a volume of Neuroscience and Behavioral Physiology. "'Interaction Between Learning and Paradoxical Sleep in Cats.'" She looked up and grinned. "Maybe he did get a cat!"

Jaxon kept on reading as he shook his head.

"There's a lot here on paradoxical sleep and other such conditions," he said, ignoring her attempt to be funny. "Parasomnia... Lucid dreaming... Hypnopompic sleep paralysis..."

"Looking for answers..." Sheridan muttered, not bothering to add the rest of the lyric, though something told her it applied. Jaxon, apparently, hadn't picked up on the vibe.

"Clearly, that's one of the reasons he took part in the research study where I met him. But there are so many other things here as well. Astral projection and ley lines and at least five different papers or studies on the Aurora Borealis."

Sheridan lifted her head at his words, her brow dipping down as her focus locked on his words.

Aurora Borealis.

The Northern Lights...

Jaxon kept talking, but she barely heard him as memory again whisked her away.

In a rough camp somewhere deep in Denali National Park, Sheridan lay staring up into the moonless sky late into the night. She ignored the sickly-sweet aroma of burning weed nearby and focused on the heavens. The only light came from above, a multitude of sparkling points bright enough to catch the eye but not enough to cast a shadow. For the first time in her life, she breathed a deep breath and relaxed. All tension drained from her body, and she felt peacefully, blissfully alone. There were others out there. Several people from the Denver area—including her—had signed up through the local community center where Sheridan worked, along with unrelated tourists who had booked this trip through their travel agents to view the Aurora Borealis.

Everyone waited with bated breath to see if the light show would begin. Sheridan knew that. Hell, she had journeyed up the mountain with them. But she still felt separate. Not yet an accepted member of the group. That didn't bother her here. And that wasn't just a lie she told herself.

Here, in this place… in this suspended moment, she had found blessed solitude.

And then, in slowly growing flickers, fire lit the sky!

Undulating curtains of translucent green billowed overhead, cascading across the heavens, with smaller ribbons of purple and blue joining the dance. Around her sounded a chorus of indrawn breaths, a few clicks followed by the whir of camera shutters, but then reverent silence.

Sheridan went still, immersed in the awe of the experience. Her eyes widened as a curious sensation rippled over her. A sensation she had felt before amplified a thousand-fold. A chill, like a current of air brushing against her skin, displaced by an opening door, but no door ever constructed by man. She had felt this each time the shadows came, when they skated along the edges of her world. Lurking at the border peering in, cloaked, as Sheridan had always imagined, behind curtain walls like those dancing above her head. Fluid and fluctuating. Sometimes touching and at others, bowing away from one another.

She tensed, every muscle locking tight, even her breath arrested. The darkness around her took on weight and depth until she felt surrounded as she had never been before. For the first time during such an occurrence, sounds teased her ears. Like the evening commute passing through New York's Grand Central Station, which she'd experienced once on a trip with her father, the sensation had stuck with her. The dull rumble as thousands passed through the terminal, intent on their destinations, only peripherally aware of those surrounding them. Enough to be annoyed or to evade, but no more. Bumping and shoving and snarling their way to their designated tracks.

That. It was like that, only with the suffocating weight of darkness crushing down on her. A darkness that had nothing to do with the absence of light.

As the light show faded from the sky, a flash of red flickered in the upper reaches, and a sense of dread like no other settled over Sheridan shattering the peace of her surroundings like a primordial cry. The muscles in her chest tightened, and she gasped for breath, unsuccessfully. What light there was dimmed, then vanished as the darkness closed in. Sheridan fought it, able to feel the tears coursing down the sides of her face and into her hair, but little else. Bone-deep, bitter cold swept over her along with such a sense of dread that she feared she faced her end on the side of a far-off mountain, surrounded but all alone.

No one would even know until morning.

Her heart cried out as consciousness slipped from her grip.

And then she saw it. A final flicker of blue flashed overhead. With it, a surge of returning warmth rippled through her body, fighting back the bone-deep chill. A glowing orb crossed above her, obscuring the sky, sparking an odd sense of recognition.

"Sheri...?" a startled voice murmured by her ear, edged with both hope and disbelief. A voice different than she remembered but just the same, somehow familiar to her befuddled mind.

On a surge of fought-for breath, Sheridan gasped back, "Mama?"

But the presence faded, and a gentler darkness drew Sheridan down to sleep.

"Hey! You in there?"

Sheridan jerked, her gaze locking with Jaxon's as he waved a hand before her eyes, trying to get her attention. She looked up at him and said, "You know, they don't only happen in the north... or even the north and south. Those are just the best places we can see them."

"What?"

"The polar lights. Aurora Borealis in the north... Aurora Australis in the south. Those are the ones that stand out, but they happen everywhere. All the time, even during the day. We just can't see them most of the time. Light pollution. Refraction. There are a number of theories. They say the lights are caused by charged particles from solar activity interacting with gases in our atmosphere, but they are just as likely to occur when there is no solar activity..."

She trailed off as she noticed Jaxon grinning at her.

"So, did something wake up your inner academic?"

A faint grimace twitched Sheridan's lip. "Just a flashback. Coming home has... woken up a lot of memories. Aurorae have always been something of a fascination of mine." One she hadn't realized her father shared.

"What were you saying?" she asked, her brow creasing as she realized she'd missed whatever Jaxon had initially said.

His earlier concern returned to his gaze. "It's getting late, and I have a lab to run tomorrow. But I'm free tomorrow night. Do you want me to take some of this with me or leave it here?"

Sheridan shook her head to that last part. "Go ahead and take it all. You're the researcher. You're much more likely to make sense out of all that. After all, you are trained for it."

Jaxon nodded. "I'll go back over the pictures we pulled down from Google Photos as well, in case we missed something. So, see you tomorrow night?" He asked as he started to slide the materials into his backpack. Something caught Sheridan's eye, distracting her from his question. Her primitive reactives... how did they end up in the pile?

"Oh! Wait." Sheridan took the bag from him, separating her childhood artwork from the other papers. When she was satisfied she had them all, she handed the rest back.

"O...kay..."

"Hush! Those are hardly scientific research. Leave the art to me."

Jaxon lifted an eyebrow, then slanted a glance at the journal. She resisted the urge to stick her tongue out at him, lest he get the wrong idea... or was that the right one... She swatted down her newly resurrected crush.

"You were leaving, right?"

With a rueful laugh, he smiled and headed for the back door. "Good night!"

"'Night!"

"Tomorrow!" he called out as he went down the steps and into the darkness. "I'll bring dinner."

She followed him, stepping out on the stoop as he got into his truck and pulled away with a final wave. As he left, part of her wanted to call him back. And not because of any lingering attraction. A shiver rippled across her skin as the silence around her took on a weighted feel. In a slow tilt, she looked up at the sky. Though only stars twinkled above, she would swear undulating curtains of green light teased the corner of her eye, accented by ribbons of blue, yellow, and purple. The ghost of a tingle tripped her nerves. A memory of Denali, or something more... immediate?

With a faint shiver, she went inside, stopping at the table where her drawings lay. She reached out a hand and slowly fanned the pages. On each one, Papa had scrawled a name and a color. Nothing else. Worrying her lip, she separated the pages, moving them side by side.

Green. Purple. Blue. White. Pink. Orange. Yellow... Red.

All the colors seen in the Aurora.

Each one with a distinct image. A particular name. All of them Shadow People? Each one from somewhere different?

She sighed and let her head fall forward. It felt significant. But it also felt like too much.

Perhaps others would call it procrastination, but tomorrow felt soon enough to come fresh to her problems. She just didn't have the energy for anything more tonight.

Chapter Sixteen

On her way back to her room, Sheridan left on every light she passed.

She set her drawings and Papa's journal beside her bed, along with her phone, then turned to the clothes she still hadn't dealt with on the floor. From the *keeping either way* pile, she extracted a comfy, cozy footless onesie she would never consider herself too old for. As she slid on the thick, plush flannel and zipped up the field of midnight blue hung with crescent moons and twinkling stars, her muscles slowly unfurled from their bunches. She made a quick trip back to the kitchen for a scoop of Forbidden Chocolate ice cream, then nestled into bed with her eBook app open on her phone. Five pages in, her eyelids fluttered, then drooped. She managed to keep them open long enough to set her phone on the nightstand and finish her treat but struggled to go brush her teeth before climbing back into her nest of blankets and turning off the light.

But sleep dodged away before her lowering eyes.

Sheridan lay there, every comfort met save for her need to know. A need she'd denied as long as other things distracted her. Sighing, she opened her eyes and stared at the ceiling to avoid looking deep into her soul.

It didn't work.

Papa knew. He knew about the shadows. Why hadn't he said anything? Why had he left her to struggle through it on her own? *Everything* on her own? Acid churned in her gut, fed by a surge of anger she had never acknowledged until now.

No child should ever be left to their own devices. No child should ever have to figure out how to deal with problems all by themselves. To feel they are different and not be reassured that that was okay. She had grown up never wanting to be a bother, never feeling she should disturb him. Knowing she was loved but feeling on her own, even when she'd lived beneath the same roof.

No child with a parent should feel that way.

Just because she'd been self-sufficient didn't mean he should have left her to raise herself.

She had the sudden need to lash out and no way to do so. Ashamed for even feeling the impulse, given Papa's condition. But that only heightened her resentment. Again, she was left to deal with things all alone.

Sheridan's breathing increased, resentful of a childhood she hadn't recognized as flawed until she reached the other side and discovered what it should have been. Could have been, if Papa had been more present. Less obsessed. Did he even realize the scars he'd given her? The scars she only now recognized. If she were honest, she'd been like a shadow in her own life. He hadn't neglected her physical needs, but emotionally? His focus had definitely been elsewhere.

Or was she just angry that she might lose him? That she might have to make the call?

Then no one would be left, and she truly would be all alone.

Closing her eyes, she shunted that realization away.

Her thoughts went back to where this had all begun: the Shadow People.

All this time, she had struggled with being different, only to find out she wasn't alone. Others had seen the shadows. Maybe had experiences similar to hers. Though, she hoped not quite. She knew what had happened to Mama and wouldn't wish that on anyone else. But were they responsible for Papa's state as well?

Huffing out a frustrated growl, she threw the blankets aside and clicked on the light. According to her phone, it was just after midnight. Sheridan eyed the journal on her nightstand and the stack of drawings beneath. She remembered the notes Papa had scribbled in the margins. If she were to do a search for "Shadow People," would she find those names, as she expected?

The journal itself might contain the answers, or it might not, but she knew one thing: this time, she wasn't going through it all alone. Over the past few weeks, she had learned that most of the nurses didn't care if she sat quietly by her father's bed, no matter the hour. He might not be able to answer—he certainly couldn't explain himself—but he would be present when she delved into his private thoughts.

She climbed from her comfortable nest with a sigh and stripped off her onesie. In more ways than one, she pulled on her big girl pants (and everything else), grabbed Papa's journal, and went to sit vigil.

When she reached the hospital and went to his floor, the lights were muted, and the night crew went about their duties in hushed tones. The patient rooms stood open, with most of the lights off or dropped down low, so Sheridan moved quietly down the hall. Kate sat at the nurses' station charting. She looked up with a nod and a faint smile, which Sheridan returned, then went back to her work.

Sheridan slipped into her father's room to discover someone had been assigned the second bed.

Part of her felt cheated. Robbed of the chance to vent her newly acknowledged resentment.

The light was off in the other bay, but the television facing that bed played low. Not wanting to disturb whoever rested there, Sheridan moved Papa's guest chair to the other side of his bed, closest to the door, then sat down, the journal closed on her lap. For a while, she just sat there cataloging the changes in her father's condition, the translucency of his skin, the way it molded tighter to his features while also somehow seeming slack, the stillness more pronounced than any visit before.

Her eyes ached with unspent tears as she fought the sudden need to curl up next to him as she had as a child, sheltering silently by his side on the couch as he poured through his research. The memory—one she cherished—tempered her earlier anger, siphoning it off until she could bear it, love and heartache returning to fill the space.

Sheridan jumped as the television facing the other bed clicked off, leaving the room shrouded in near darkness. Reaching over, she twisted the flexible reading lamp over Papa's bed toward her and pulled it low, wincing at the loud *click* as she turned it on.

An expectant hush filled the space. She took up the journal, feathered open the pages, and began to read at random, the beginning being too painful with her heart so raw.

Chapter Seventeen

Thud.

Sheridan jerked awake at the sudden noise, wincing as she looked around her, stiff neck protesting. Papa lay unmoved beside her while someone shifted in the bed beyond. A hint of sunlight filtered through the far window, casting the other patient's shadow against the dividing curtain. Visible. Distorted. Signs of life, but separate, like a glimpse into another world.

A passage from the journal surfaced in Sheridan's memory: *There can be no shadow without light... no light without shadow...* She would argue that point if only her father were able to debate her back.

"Hey..." a woman's voice called out softly.

Smothering a cry as her head snapped toward the sound, Sheridan discovered Kate leaning in the door.

"Oh. Hey."

Kate looked out the door and then back again. "Sorry, the morning shift will be arriving soon. You should go."

Sheridan nodded, frowning as she looked around for the journal.

"It's by your feet."

"Thanks," Sheridan whispered, but Kate was already gone.

Picking up the book, Sheridan leaned over her father as she straightened. "Love you, Papa," she murmured as she brushed a kiss across his cheek, his skin papery against her lips. "I have to go, but I'll be back later."

She almost left the book behind. Other than insight into a grieving husband at a loss on how to parent alone, she hadn't gleaned much from those pages. Well, nothing that would help her now. Early entries mentioned Sheridan had been distraught and progressively agitated. She'd insisted Mama had been abducted by a "shadowy man," falling into violent tantrums when no one would get her mother back. In the end, they had sedated her, for lack of a better word, giving her something called Diazepam for what Papa termed anxiety.

Great start on the parenting, Papa. Don't deal with the feelings. Shut them off.

Of course, who was she to judge? How could she expect a man at such a loss to think clearly? Still, Sheridan would have to read up on the drug and see what the long-term effects were. It could explain a lot.

In the end, she held on to the journal as she left Papa's hospital room, planning to return it to the shelf in his study with all the others.

There were so many. Perhaps she'd just started with the wrong one?

Just as she reached the elevator, a commotion sounded at her back. Harsh buzzing. Raised voices, the slap of cushioned soles running in the opposite direction. Sheridan stopped and turned to see a stream of medical personnel disappear into her father's room. Before realizing she'd moved, she found herself back in his doorway, staring on as they clustered around his bed.

"Epinephrine, stat!"

"Someone get this chair out of here."

"What's his BP?"

"I can't find a big enough vein. Get that ultrasound in here, now!"

The staff moved in carefully choreographed chaos, the sounds of their rapid-fire chatter blending together until Sheridan could make no sense of it. She watched on, unnoticed, her chest tightening as their efforts continued. Her body swayed, jostled as people came and went from the room.

"Miss! Miss! You have to move. You can't be here."

Sheridan blinked and barely looked away from her father, her breath coming in pants.

"Someone take her out of the way, damn it! This isn't a show!"

She barely felt the pressure as one of the staff gripped her arm and started tugging her from the room, but as soon as she did, as soon as her line of sight broke, Sheridan dug in.

"No! That's my father!" She struggled and pulled back, afraid to lose sight of him, afraid that if she did, he would be gone from her life forever. That she would have failed him.

Whoever tried to lead her away gave a sharp pull.

"NO!"

A stinging slap landed across Sheridan's cheek.

"Do you want them to save him or not?" Kate snapped at her. "Let them do their jobs."

Sheridan's mouth dropped open, and the fight went out of her. Her eyes burned and her vision blurred as tears etched a path down her face. Her lower lip trembled as she tried to speak, but she lost the words before her mouth could form them.

"Come on, let's get you settled."

As Kate slid an arm around her and led her away, Sheridan glanced back, her brow furrowing at a gleaming glow that seemed to hover above the crash team working over her father.

"The chapel or the waiting room?" Kate asked, her tone low and soothing now that Sheridan cooperated. She turned toward Kate, but part of her couldn't make sense of the question. The look of compassion on the nurse's face jarred Sheridan back to the surface enough to speak.

"What?"

Kate tried again. "Where do you want to wait, the chapel or the waiting room?"

Sheridan worked to focus on her choice, despite the tumult still heard at her back. "Whichever is closer."

Nodding, Kate turned and headed for what looked like a private sitting room further down the hall, just past a second nurses' station. It looked like a repurposed closet, barely six feet wide with two armchairs facing one another and a soothing water feature burbling on an accent table in front of the window. The blinds were drawn, and two standing lamps created the illusion of a comfortable space. Each chair sat within reach of the table, a selection of religious texts, and a box of tissues.

Illusion blown.

"Why don't you settle in here? Someone will come to you as soon as there's any word."

It took an effort to walk into that narrow room and sit down in the floral chintz armchair that looked like it belonged in a grandmother's sitting room. Numbness settled over Sheridan as she fixed her eyes on the door.

"Can I bring you water? Or tea?"

Sheridan shuddered and shook her head, barely noticing as Kate turned and went her way, leaving the door open.

After a time, the atmosphere on the floor calmed and resumed its normal harried pace, but still, no one came. Sheridan was about to get up when Dr. Varughese appeared in the doorway, his hand resting on the knob. Though the morning had barely begun, he looked worn, and Sheridan's grip tightened on the arms of her chair as she noted the grim set to his lips.

"Good morning, Ms. Cascaden."

As her impulse was to say, *not hardly*, Sheridan nodded in acknowledgment but remained silent.

"Do you mind if I close the door?"

Her grip tightened even more. "No."

He stepped in the rest of the way, shutting the door gently behind him. Sheridan followed him with her gaze as he moved to the chair facing hers. Before he sat, he drew something out of the pocket of his lab coat.

"Nurse McAllister found this on the floor outside your father's room."

Her father's journal.

Sheridan just stared at it, wondering if she was too late.

"How is my father?" she asked, startled at how broken her voice sounded in the small, enclosed room.

Dr. Varughese set the journal on the table beside her, then sat down.

"For now," he said, carefully neutral. "Stable."

"But?"

The doctor let out a long breath. "His body is failing, bit by bit, faster than we expected. It is all we can do to maintain him..." His words trailed off as he left the rest of his statement unsaid.

Sheridan heard it anyway, but she wasn't ready to make that call.

Slowly standing, she picked up the journal and released a quavering sigh.

Dr. Varughese scrambled to stand with her, his manners clearly ingrained.

"Thank you, doctor. And please thank the staff for their efforts."

Holding her head high and forcing every step, Sheridan returned to her father's room and moved to stand beside his bed. No longer concerned with who may or may not hear, she said what she had come to say.

"I love you, Papa. You're a crappy father, but you're mine, and if I can figure out how to bring you back, we *will* do better."

She didn't remember leaving the hospital or driving home, but somehow, she got there.

Chapter Eighteen

Entering the kitchen through the back door, Sheridan was struck by the silence. The house fairly vibrated with it. As if something loomed expectant for her return. Glowering, she flicked on the under-the-counter radio as she passed, twisting the volume until it would twist no more. Quiet Riot blared through the cheap speakers, waking up the house for what felt like the first time in forever.

Before she could overthink things, Sheridan powered through the house, heading straight for the study. In defiance, she left the door wide open and crossed the room to the shelf of journals. Squatting, she looked for the open slot for the journal in her hand. She replaced it on the shelf and counted back to the one from '96, the year before she'd been born. She plucked that one from the shelf and lowered her body the rest of the way to the ground, sitting cross-legged as she wandered through the account of her parents' early years. If not for the reason that brought her here, she would have smiled as she savored each page.

If not for the reason...

Instead, she tore through each entry headfirst until she hit an unexpected wall, crashing hard until every bit of her felt broken.

Mary died tonight; Papa wrote. *I swear on my life, she died.*

I know it sounds crazy, and I can't explain it, but she had a seizure while we were night hiking in the foothills, hoping to catch a rare glimpse of the Northern Lights in our southward sky. Some kind of fit struck Mary down, and nothing I did made a difference. I felt the life go out of her. And yet, as I cradled her still form and waited for help to come, the Lights lit the sky, and something buzzed through us both like a faint electric charge. When I looked down, Mary stared up at me, dazed, disoriented, but alive!

Sheridan groaned and dropped the book. She raised her hands to her head and tried to rub a growing tension headache away. If she never read that her mother had died *again*, it would be too soon. But the rest of it... she couldn't explain it any more than her father had, but this was the key. This was the point of transition between Richard's Mary and Sheridan's Mama. It had to be.

And the Lights. The Aurora.

Threads to the puzzle, all falling into place.

At first, Papa kept coming back to *Something's different. Mary isn't herself.* But gradually, those references fell away as they discovered Mary was pregnant, and anticipation grew for Sheridan herself. Of course, after Mary was gone, all joy fled Papa's words as first grief and then obsession took over.

It broke her heart to read, but Sheridan snatched up the journal and the next one and the next until none were left. She slumped forward, shuddering as the last book slipped from her fingers, feeling thrashed and battered to her very soul.

She had her answers, but at the cost of witnessing Papa's spiraling decline, documented in his own hand, his mad obsession with getting his Mary back from what he called the Shadow Realm. Another dimension among many dimensions existing in concert with their own.

Most would call the journals Richard's decent into madness. True or not, she couldn't say, but for Papa, he had cleaved to his theory like the gospel, and he the staunchest disciple.

And he believed Sheridan was the key.

When she was younger, she had had such vivid dreams. Hyperlucid, Papa called them in one of the journals. Dreams beyond this world, literally. Where he believed she journeyed from her subconscious across dimensions in a way no one had even theorized before. Whether she believed his interpretation or not, she couldn't say, but part of her remembered this... seeking out her shadow friends and discovering whole new realms. She remembered *now*, she should say, but that part had slumbered a long time. Since her mother's disappearance, in fact.

Sheridan suspected it had been the Diazepam, but how would she ever know? And should she accept those memories as fact or fancy? Closing her eyes, she searched within, examined her experiences, both past and present, and as insane as it sounded, she felt at peace with fact.

According to the journal, Papa couldn't explain how she had journeyed, but once he'd latched on to the idea Mama had *gone away*, not *passed away*, he'd been desperate to replicate the experience himself. Psychotropic drugs, meditation, astral projection. Hell, even electroshock. Papa tried it all and more. But only on himself. Though he believed Sheridan had shown the way, the fear of further loss drove him to separate his daughter from the process.

Something must have worked, but Sheridan would be damned if she knew what he'd done. As far as she could tell, he hadn't figured it out for at least another four journals, each one more disjointed than the last. In the end, it seemed he barely remained lucid in the waking world, let alone in his dreams.

How had she not noticed? Guilt sank roots into her gut, twisting them.

Sheridan returned the journal she'd been skimming to the shelf and climbed to her feet.

Papa might have thrashed about in the dark, but she knew the way. Or at least, she had.

She left the study and headed for her room, barely noticing that Led Zeppelin now rocked the house over the radio. Behind her, Papa's pendulum clock chimed three times, jolting her as she realized more than half the day had passed unnoticed. Moving with a purpose, she turned off all the lights as she passed, inviting the shadows instead of chasing them away.

As she entered the hallway, Sheridan slowed, then stopped, her eyes tracking the wires and lights festooning the walls. Instead of going to her own room, she turned and entered Papa's, laying herself on the bed like a willing lab rat seeking the cheese.

Deep and slow, she breathed. Deep and slow. She willed her muscles to relax and her mind to clear. Part of her noted how much easier this had been as a child when will trounced nearly everything. But adult Sheridan fought distraction and worry, struggled to achieve calm, the gateway to focus.

When she had silenced everything and hovered on the cusp of sleep, she turned her thoughts to her parents, and love and longing sought them out.

A growing light shimmered before her eyes, shifting and undulating in increasing waves. Mostly green, but that wasn't right. It didn't feel right. Each color led somewhere different. When Sheridan thought of Mama, it felt blue, a bright, happy blue sparkling with starlight.

An azure thread appeared, winding and flexing around the green until it settled at her feet, rising like a curtain before a door. Sheridan reached out, ran her hand across the surface, and watched it dance, feeling a warm sizzle along her fingertips.

She laughed, and something moved beyond the curtain, alert and turning her way. A graceful silhouette drew closer, raising a hand as if to meet Sheridan's, only to hesitate, poised dark against the light. On instinct, Sheridan stepped up, hands forward as if to part the curtain, only to pass straight through a dazzling sheet of light.

A gasp greeted her. Sheridan blinked, then smiled, tears pricking her eyes as she met Mama's gaze, the same but different. Though she longed to throw herself forward, she held back. What if this wasn't real? Her heart would bleed dry if that were true... But... Mama...

"Mama..."

A smile as dazzling as the light lit Mama's face.

Sheridan reached out slowly in the barest touch, sending a trail of sparks across her mother's cheek. A gasp escaped Sheridan's lips as their substance melded for an instant. Her head tilted, and she felt her eyes widen as she met Mama's gaze.

"This is a realm of energy," Mama said, though Sheridan hadn't asked the question. "Thought is form, but all is energy and interacts accordingly."

Sheridan nodded, understanding the words, if not the concept, so foreign to her reality. In the end, it didn't matter. They were there. Together.

"Oh, I missed you!" she laughed, unable to take her eyes from her mother.

"And I missed you, so very much."

At those words, Sheridan teared up and looked away, blinking to clear them. Her mouth fell open as she took in their surroundings, like a pastel... no... like a watercolor created with light. For a moment, she let herself get lost in the experience, all of her senses engaged, somehow triggered in distinctly different ways by the cascade of energy surrounding her... When it became too much, she closed her eyes and stepped back, reaching for the calm she'd strove for earlier.

"Papa?" she asked, speaking toward where she felt Mama... standing, like a warm ray of sunlight pouring through glass. *Interesting,* she thought, as the beam noticeably cooled. She opened her eyes to look at her mother.

"He says, he's sorry. For everything. He didn't realize..." Mama answered, her hand waving toward a faintly glowing orb Sheridan hadn't yet noticed, weaker than Mama's warmth, almost lost among the light cascading around them.

"Oh, Papa, what have you done?" she murmured, feeling her own energy dim. "What have *I* done?"

Mama smiled, projecting reassurance. "You have nothing to fear."

"How? How is this possible?"

"You are my true daughter, and this is my world. Once you discovered the way, it was always open to you. But the other world, that's still yours, and nothing can keep you from it."

"How?" Sheridan repeated, the single word quavering.

Mama looked down, fluxing as if to flinch.

"That I can't tell you. I don't even know how I crossed myself... that first time. I was afraid, desperate. I needed to protect you..." She fell silent a moment, without saying from what. "Somehow, I found a gap that let me through, but that gap closed, and I never did feel it again. I couldn't return if I'd wanted to."

Sheridan gasped. The thought had never occurred to her that Mama might have left them on purpose. The possibility pierced her heart like a thorn. "But you did," she ground out through clenched teeth, sparking like an exposed wire.

Slowly, Mama shook her head. "Never. Not by choice. I fought to stay with you and your father with everything I had, but that was not my place, and the more my energy drained away, the less I could fight those who would draw me back."

"How did Papa do it?"

Mama frowned, her lip twitching almost in a snarl. "Your *father*," she said in a tight voice, her gaze flickering to the orb hovering by her shoulder, "did a very foolish thing, and we all must live with the consequences because nothing that I know can return him to his plane, with his anchor cut away."

The words hit Sheridan like a physical blow.

"So... he will die?" she whispered, half statement, half question.

A twitch of Mama's head served as a nod. "His body, yes. But not his essence, though I don't know how long that will sustain this form. It's never been done, that I know of."

Sheridan drew a deep breath and slowly released it. Her gaze went from parent to parent against this surreal landscape of light and color and energy. *Is there a place for me here? Might we stay together and fix what has broken between us?*

She feared to ask.

In the end, she didn't have to. She flinched away from Mama's knowing look.

"You should go. There are those who would harm you for what you are."

"What am I, Mama?"

"A soul with no anchor to restrict you. A creature not bound to a dimension. Where you will, you go, and to some, there is nothing more dangerous."

Memories of the Shadow Man rose up. He'd come for Mama. He'd even come for Sheridan. What was to stop him from doing so again?

"The pendant. The one you gave me. Is it really a protection?"

Mama shot her a sly grin and shook her head. "Protection from yourself."

Sheridan furrowed her brow, and the currents dimmed.

"Sorry. It is an anchor. It kept me with you, and it kept you grounded, so you didn't wander off and accidentally find the bad shadow the way you'd sought out your… friends."

Here Mama's grin softened into a sparkling smile. "The way you found me…"

"Then how do I stop the Shadow Man?"

"He cannot cross the border curtain. He can lurk, and he can loom, but he cannot hurt you. He cannot force you where you do not want to go. Don't let him trick you. Don't give him that power over you."

"I won't."

Mama's smile faded away. "You have to go."

Barely whispering the words, Sheridan asked, "Can I come back? Sometimes? Can I visit when I miss you too much?"

Papa's orb bobbed as if to say yes, but Mama frowned, her eyes shimmering.

"For now… it's too dangerous. Give it some time. We'll figure this out. For now, go back and build a life for yourself. And for god's sake, put my house back the way it should be!"

Sheridan barked a laugh, which shot up, then rained down like fireworks, and she dipped her head once. Then, before she lost the chance, she darted forward and clung to her mother, tensing as they melded everywhere their surfaces touched, warmth glowing fiercely from the join. "I love you."

"I'm here," Mama murmured back nearly thought to thought, brushing her lips across Sheridan's brow, but even as she said it, the words faded and wavered, and Sheridan woke in Papa's bed, her back arching with a sob like no other before. She fell back, spent, and let the tears flow down her face and through her hair and across her pillow.

Chapter Nineteen

The room fell first into shadow, then into darkness, and still, Sheridan lay there spent, the music from the kitchen a muted rumble nearly drowned out by the raging in her head. For hours she reached for the calm she'd achieved earlier, knowing she would need it for what came next.

For hours, she failed.

All Sheridan achieved was a state of numbness, gone in an instant at the feel of something landing on her bed, soft... light... but there when nothing should be. She jerked upright, a yell shattering the stillness surrounding her like a bubble. As she whipped her head around, a patch of solid darkness disappeared down the hallway in silence. Gritting her teeth, Sheridan propelled herself from the bed in pursuit, anger and hurt twisting her expression, locking in on this intrusion in proxy of the one that caused it.

She cursed as she clipped walls and stumbled over furniture blended with the shadows. And still, she followed the flicker of movement, more sensed than seen, until she hit the kitchen.

There, frozen in a beam of moonlight, a lean black cat stared up at her as if trying to decide which way to go.

"Oh!" Sheridan gasped, then she started to laugh, spooking the little puss worse than before. It scrambled across the tile and headed toward the basement door emitting a high-pitched cry before disappearing into nothingness, though there was nowhere it could have gone. Smacking on the light, Sheridan peered where the cat had darted. This time she roared, the laughter ringing a bit hysterical as tears rolled down her face. Sliding to the floor, she stared at a tiny cut-out she hadn't noticed in the door, covered by a little brown flap that blended into the wood. Two bright yellow eyes stared back at her from under the slightly raised edge.

As she sat there, both laughing and crying, the radio kicked into the Ramones, and she laughed harder until she couldn't see for the tears.

She jerked and cried out as a heavy mass slammed into the back door, startling the cat back down the basement stairs. Another impact. And twice more. Too fast for her to scramble away, the door crashed open with the tearing sound of splintering wood.

Jaxon stumbled into the kitchen, panic in his gaze as he scanned the room for threats.

"What's wrong? What happened? Is it Richard?" The questions just tumbled from his lips. "I kept knocking and calling, and you wouldn't answer. Like you couldn't even hear me."

Sheridan looked up at him and just shook her head, too weary to explain. Not quite sure if she even could. She waved him off as he tried to search her for injuries.

"Just hold me," she mumbled, mortified as a hiccup broke her words. Jaxon stilled and didn't ask why. He lowered himself the rest of the way to the floor and folded his body around hers, lightly rubbing her arm. They stayed that way for hours until Sheridan couldn't tell whose heartbeat was whose and until surely, Jaxon could hardly tell she'd been crying.

"Want to talk about it?" he finally asked, his words gentle and low, spoken into the fall of her hair.

"Nope. Not tonight."

He nodded and held her a little tighter.

"Probably not tomorrow either," she added. "Or the next."

"But someday?" he quipped.

"Maybe… You'll have to stick around to find out."

Jaxon stilled, then resumed stroking her arm. "Not a problem."

Sheridan smiled and snuggled against him.

"Oh… Apparently… I *am* a weirdo freak."

Jaxon gave her a little shake in his arms, frowning down at her. "Unique, not freak."

She ignored him, more comfortable in her freakiness than she had ever been.

"Aaand… Also, apparently, Papa did get a cat," she said with a chuckle as the little black floof crept through the makeshift cat door and settled in her lap.

They stayed that way through the night because it felt right, and Sheridan didn't feel like moving. Tomorrow, she would make the call. Tomorrow, they would set the house to order.

Right now, Sheridan was *not* alone, and nothing else mattered.

artist's rendition of a Shadow Person (Hat Man)

Shadow People

(Also known as *Hat Man, The Hooded Monk, Old Hag, Black Smoke People, Peeking Shadows, Red-Eyed Shadows, Tariaksuq, The Watchers, Mist People,* and various other names worldwide.)

ORIGINS: While the theories abound, nothing definitive has been settled on as the origin of the Shadow People. Some of the most popular theories on the nature and origin of Shadow People are as follows:

They are other-dimensional beings; they are time travelers; they are the early stage of emergent demons; they are guardian angels; they are developing doppelgangers; they are extraterrestrial in nature; they are the aura of an individual scrying the victim.

From a scientific rationale, Shadow People are hallucinations stemming from several possible scenarios. The first is sleep paralysis, or Paradoxical Sleep, where chemicals in the brain freeze the body's muscles during REM sleep so that the sleeper does not physically act out their dreams during sleep. A person can wake before the chemicals have cleared from their body. Sleep paralysis can occur when falling asleep or waking and produces the symptoms conversant with a visitation. The second is Pareidolia, the human mind's ability to see shapes or pictures in randomness.

Some theorize these effects are caused by the abuse of the stimulant methamphetamine, which — due to prolonged sleep deprivation — can be the cause of hallucinations matching the description of Shadow People, or mental conditions such as schizophrenia or bipolar disorder, which can cause a similar perception of shadowy figures in the subject's peripheral vision. There are even some theories that this effect is caused by sound, or to be precise, infrasound, which is of low enough frequency that the human ear cannot hear it but is known to affect both mind and body.

DESCRIPTION: Accounts depict the Shadow People as solid black humanoid masses that appear at the foot of the bed or in the corner of the room. Height varies from child-sided to taller than normal. They move with fast, jerky motions and can pass through solid matter, often disappearing through walls or mirrors. Some wear hats, and some wear cloaks. All basically have a human shape but are only defined from the waist up. The legs generally fade in an approximation of those appendages to the floor. When they are seen moving, they have been described as gliding rather than walking.

In most cases, the Shadow Person is featureless, like a silhouette but with substance, though some accounts mention the beings as semi-transparent.

If a feature is mentioned, it is generally the eyes, which can be of varying colors, perhaps linked to the particular nature of that entity, such as red eyes being malevolent and white eyes being benevolent. To this effect, some believe Shadow People are actually demonic beings, and the more powerful they get, the less distinct their shape becomes.

Though there is no indication of Shadow People attempting to verbally communicate, some say that if you look at their chest or eyes, they scream, making a sound like static, wind, or wood creaking.

Reports have been documented of a great sense of fear or malevolence. Whether this stems from the creature or the experience is unclear. Some people feel the Shadow People are parasitic beings there to feed off of fear; others believe they are guardian spirits that mean no harm.

It is common in the accounts where the person has the experience during sleep to exhibit paralysis and heaviness, including difficulty breathing as if they are being smothered or someone is on their chest. In many cases, those reporting the encounter express being overcome with a sense of dread or fear. Others have had a sensation of having someone sit beside them, having their blankets pulled away, or being touched. Some say they have a black spot where they were touched that did not go away for years.

In almost all cases, the person experiencing the visitation described only being watched, with the Shadow Person going when they were noticed.

There have also been cases reported of people observing Shadow People, or occasionally Shadow Animals, in the daylight hours, both inside and outside. Such as hiding behind a bush or moving down stairs. Some cases of sightings seem tied to a particular location, but others seem tied to an individual, with the episodes following them sometimes clear to other states.

Another variation equated with Shadow People is a glowing white orb that will likewise disappear by passing through solid matter.

LIFE CYCLE: Undetermined.

HISTORY: Shadow People are one of the first identified cryptids in recorded history, with sightings documented for thousands of years worldwide, with variants found in every culture and religion. Those accounts show startling similarity, regardless of period or location.

In 1887, the French author Guy de Maupassant wrote the story "Le Horla" about shadow beings with similarities to depictions of Shadow People.

The term was first used in 1953 as the title of a radio drama broadcast on a popular Chicago station. In April 2001, another late-night radio show revitalized the belief in Shadow People, and later that year, a book titled *The Secret War* was written about them.

As recent as 2010, Shadow People were the most regularly reported paranormal occurrence in America.

POSSIBLE VARIATIONS: Some of the cryptids Shadow People have also been equated with are the Bogeyman, the Raven Mocker, and the Djinn, all creatures that take black, shadowy form.

About the Author

Award-winning author, editor, and publisher Danielle Ackley-McPhail has worked both sides of the publishing industry for longer than she cares to admit. In 2014, she joined forces with Mike McPhail and Greg Schauer to form eSpec Books.

Her published works include seven novels, *Yesterday's Dreams, Tomorrow's Memories, Today's Promise, The Halfling's Court, The Redcaps' Queen, Daire's Devils,* and *Baba Ali and the Clockwork Djinn,* written with Day Al-Mohamed. She is also the author of the solo collections *Eternal Wanderings, A Legacy of Stars, Consigned to the Sea, Flash in the Can, Transcendence, Between Darkness and Light, The Fox's Fire, The Kindly One,* and the non-fiction writers' guides *The Literary Handyman, More Tips from the Handyman,* and *LH: Build-A-Book Workshop.* She is the senior editor of the *Bad-Ass Faeries* anthology series, *Gaslight & Grimm, Side of Good/Side of Evil, After Punk,* and *Footprints in the Stars.* Her short stories are included in over fifty other anthologies and collections.

In addition to her literary acclaim, she crafts and sells original costume horns under the moniker The Hornie Lady Custom Costume Horns, and homemade flavor-infused candied ginger under the brand of Ginger KICK! at literary conventions, on commission, and wholesale.

Danielle lives in New Jersey with husband and fellow writer Mike McPhail and four extremely spoiled cats.

Her work can be found online at https://especbooks.square.site.

About the Artist

Although Jason Whitley has worn many creative hats, he is at heart a traditional illustrator and painter. With author James Chambers, Jason collaborates and illustrates the sometimes-prose, sometimes graphic novel, *The Midnight Hour,* which is being collected into one volume by eSpec Books. His and Scott Eckelaert's newspaper comic strip, Sea Urchins, has been collected into four volumes. Along with eSpec Books' Systema Paradoxa series, Jason is working on a crime noir graphic novel. His portrait of Charlotte Hawkins Brown is on display in the Charlotte Hawkins Brown Museum.

CAPTURE THE CRYPTIDS!

Cryptid Crate is a monthly subscription box filled with various cryptozoology and paranormal themed items to wear, display and collect. Expect a carefully curated box filled with creeptastic pieces from indie makers and artisans pertaining to bigfoot, sasquatch, UFOs, ghosts, and other cryptid and mysterious creatures (apparel, decor, media, etc).

http://CryptidCrate.com

CPSIA information can be obtained
at www.ICGtesting.com
Printed in the USA
JSHW021139280522
26340JS00002B/10